Evald Flisar

LOOK THROUGH THE WINDOW

*Translated from the Slovene
by David Limon*

Sodobnost International
2020

LOOK THROUGH THE WINDOW
Copyright © Evald Flisar, 2020
Translation copyright © David Limon, 2020

Originally published in Slovenia (European Union) as *Poglej skozi okno*
(Ljubljana: Sodobnost International, 2019).

This edition published in the United Kingdom by
Sodobnost International
www.sodobnost.com

Editor
Jana Bauer

Sub-editor
Trevor Morris

Cover design
Alen Bauer

The names, characters, and events portrayed in these pages are the product of the author's imagination. Any resemblance to actual persons, living or dead, or to real events is entirely coincidental.

All rights reserved. Duplication or reproduction by any mechanical or electronic means is strictly prohibited, except for brief quotation by a reviewer, critic, or friend, or by use of Sodobnost International to publicize the work.

ISBN 978-961-7047-61-5

Orders:

Central Books, 50 Freshwater Road, Chadwell Heath, London RM8 1RX
Telephone: +44 (0) 20 8525 8800
Email: orders@centralbooks.com
www.centralbooks.com and PubEasy

Representatives:

GLOBAL BOOK MARKETING Ltd, Central Books Building, Freshwater Road, Chadwell Heath, London, England RM8 1RX
Telephone: +44 (0)20 8590 9700

Co-funded by the
Creative Europe Programme
of the European Union

The European Commission support for the production of this publication does not constitute an endorsement of the contents which reflects the views only of the authors, and the Commission cannot be held responsible for any use which may be made of the information contained therein

For Martin

1.
Early one Sunday morning

Look through the window.
Focus on the nearest apple tree.
Can you see the man leaning against it?
No? Press your forehead to the glass.
Now you see him. He's leaning against the tree and looking at the house. His posture tells you that he has come here for a reason.
The day is breaking, but the light is still weak and so you can't make out his features. Mum and dad are downstairs, in their bedroom; they like to have a lie-in on Sundays.
Who could it be at this early hour?
A refugee who has swum across the River Kolpa?
Very unlikely. Refugees come to houses in groups. There are women and children. They ask for food and water.
They are different from the man under the tree.
When they find out that the narrow road past the house goes on for only another two hundred metres and then narrows into a path, which continues into the woods where there are bears lurking, they turn around and come back.

On the road beside the Kolpa, they are sooner or later picked up by the police.

No, the man leaning against the tree is not a refugee.

He's probably waiting for a light to come on in the house, which would mean that someone is up. Of all the possibilities, this seems the most plausible. Although mum and dad have few acquaintances and even fewer friends, this man under the apple tree must be someone they know.

But why did he come at dawn on a Sunday morning?

People come visiting around midday, perhaps in the afternoon or the evening, especially on a Sunday. But never at dawn. The figure under the apple tree, indistinct and motionless, fills you with fear.

You feel like you're losing the ground beneath your feet. Like your heart has slipped into your stomach and is now bouncing around there instead of beating as it does normally.

Do something.

Run down the stairs to the ground floor, bang on the bedroom door, wake up mum and dad and tell them that a stranger is watching the house.

You half decide that's what you will do.

But then the man moves and walks towards the house. You see he's coming to the door.

Any moment now he'll ring the doorbell.

Will you open the door? Or will you wake up mum and dad?

They're never happy if you get them out of bed on a Sunday morning by making a lot of noise. This usually happens when you put on the television to count the bodies in a crime series or a war film, without turning down the volume. But you can't turn down the volume until you've turned on the television. And if the night before it was turned off by mum, who is a bit deaf and has the volume at 43, you can't avoid the deafening noise.

Of course, you quickly lower the volume, but by then it's already too late.
And you're told off. By mum.
Dad never says anything.

Look through the window.
The man is coming closer, any moment now he'll be at the door. You can see his face. It's long, with a large nose, eyes without eyebrows and a high forehead; he's not quite bald but has small tufts of hair randomly scattered around his skull.
How would you describe his face?
Cruel? Although you don't understand the real meaning of this word, which mum often uses if she happens to go past as you're watching a film where people are killing each other and are nearly all dead by the end.
'How can you watch films like that day after day?' she says.
Adding: 'Look at him, he's got such a cruel face.'
Dad doesn't say much. When films are on television, he reads a newspaper or a book.
Just once he said: 'Ten times as many people have died so far on television as in all the wars from the beginning of time.'
'You'd know,' mum said with a grimace, 'you, who knows everything and can't stand the fact that other people know a little, too.'
You found mum's words a little cruel. At that moment, you thought for the first time that you perhaps understood the meaning of that word.
And now, when you can see the face of the man who will soon be on the doorstep and press the doorbell, you don't know what to do. There's chaos in your head.

Should you lurch down the stairs to the bedroom and wake up mum and dad, and then let them decide what to do about the visitor? Or is it better to leave the responsibility for waking mum and dad to the stranger when he rings the doorbell?

You can't decide. As usual.

Choosing between this or that option is the hardest thing for you. Always has been. Again, you feel glued to the floor, unable to move.

Waiting for the strange visitor to ring the bell.

In vain. What's wrong? Has the bell stopped working overnight? Or was the stranger not visiting, but just walking past. Perhaps going next door? Or he was just a weirdo out walking at an unusual hour.

That's it, you think.

Or he would have rung the bell.

But then you hear what sounds like the front door opening. Has the stranger walked into the house because the door is unlocked? Mum usually locks it before going to bed. But sometimes she asks you to lock it when you finish watching television and go to bed.

Did she ask you last night?

You have problems remembering. At times, you remember lots of things, especially remote events, but you find it difficult to remember things from a few days ago.

Did you forget to lock the front door?

But it doesn't matter anymore.

The stranger has come into the house.

2.
What to do?

Should you grab the knife hidden under your bed? Should you rush downstairs to defend mum and dad against the evil stranger? Isn't it your duty to save their lives?

But then they would see the knife that you stole from the kitchen and are now hiding under your bed just in case the monsters you dream about every night climb in through the window.

You lied when they asked you if you knew where the knife had gone. Even though you were tempted to confess, you didn't; your fear of the monsters was too great.

If you now rushed downstairs with a knife in your hand and stabbed the stranger in the back, mum and dad would find out that you'd lied to them.

And they'd punish you.

Maybe they wouldn't let you watch television.

Or worse, they could send you to a home where they look after special needs children, a label you have been given by people called experts.

That's one reason you've got to do something!

Strange sounds are coming from downstairs. Has someone opened the bedroom door? You think you heard the hinges creak. Carefully, with the knife behind your back, you step onto the first stair. From there, you can see the hall.

The stranger is standing near the front door – sharpening a knife! Not an ordinary, kitchen knife, but a much bigger one, a butcher's knife!

Where did he get the knife sharpener? He must have brought it with him, hidden in his pocket. But the knife? It's too big to be put in a pocket. He can't have brought it with him, where did he get it from? If you attack him with your knife, you don't stand a chance since he will slaughter you with his.

And then – something strange happens!

Your dad appears in the hall, fully dressed and also holding a butcher's knife! Not as big as the one being sharpened by the stranger, but bigger than yours. Dad and the stranger obviously know each other as they exchange a few words.

What is happening?

Maybe you're still asleep, maybe this is a nightmare.

But no: when you gently stab the tip of the knife in your hand, it hurts and blood comes out. And the blood is real, so is the pain. Which means that what is happening downstairs in the hall can't be a dream.

Look!

The stranger and dad have swapped knives and the stranger is now sharpening dad's knife.

What you wouldn't give to be able to understand this!

Why don't you shout: 'Dad, what's happening?'

You daren't. You know very well that you'd get one of the following answers: 'Go back to bed!' or 'Nothing important.'

That's why you daren't ask what's happening. All you know is that you'll try to protect mum and dad if necessary. That's your duty.

You grip the knife in your right hand and get ready.

And what happens?

Something you weren't expecting. The stranger and dad, each holding a knife, go out into the yard. They leave the door half open.

Half a minute later, mum appears in the hall, also dressed, with a scarf around her neck. She's holding the plastic bowl she usually puts the washing in before hanging it to dry. Mum also goes out.

She carefully closes the front door after her.

Carefully, so as not to wake you?

You run along the landing towards the upstairs bathroom and open the door of the room on the left. The room is full of junk, but from it you can see the yard.

Look through the window.

The stranger with his butcher's knife and dad with the slightly smaller knife are walking to the wooden shed, where your friend Piggy lives. Mum is walking just behind them with the plastic bowl.

That's just coincidence, it must be; they'll go past the lean-to and into the vineyard behind it; the grapes are ripe, they'll use the sharpened knives to cut the bunches of grapes and throw them into the bowl that mum is carrying.

But is it really grape-picking time?

In the middle of the summer? Impossible.

You try to remember which month it is.

You've always had problems with this. And with days; you never know whether it's Monday, Tuesday or one of the others. But you managed to solve the problem!

13

On the wall of your room, you keep the calendar mum and dad get every year from the firefighters. Before going to bed, you mark every day with a cross and that's how you know when January begins and ends, and all the other months till the end of the year, when the firefighters bring a new calendar.

But now you're not in your room. Now you're in the room opposite yours, because you want to see what's happening in the yard. If you return to your room to see which day it is and which month, you may miss what's going on in front of the house.

But curiosity makes you go and look at the calendar.

You see that someone has circled 13 August.

And added: *Your fifteenth birthday.*

3.
Murder in the yard

Impossible! How did you manage to survive for so many years without noticing? But most people celebrate their birthday every year; how is it possible that you forgot the previous ones?
How will you celebrate your fifteenth?
Will mum bake you a cake? Will dad buy you a present? What kind of cake will it be? What will dad buy you?
Your thoughts are interrupted by a strange sound from the yard.
If someone asked you to name the sound, you'd describe it as squealing, howling, screaming, wheezing, coughing, panting and everything connected with these words.
It's clear to you what is happening.
The stranger and dad, each with his knife, are killing mum. You imagine one stabbing her in the back and the other one in the heart, then the first one in the eyes and the other one in the neck.

Quickly go to the room from which you can see the yard! Look through the window.

No one is killing mum. Something worse is happening.

The stranger and dad are pulling Piggy from his sty. The stranger grabs him by his hind legs and swiftly pulls him from the sty. Dad grabs Piggy by his front legs and helps the stranger to lay him on his side.

The stranger cuts Piggy's throat with his big knife.

Blood spurts out.

Not onto the ground, because mum has placed the washing bowl beneath him. The blood splashes into it. First in strong spurts and then in drips. When mum removes the bowl, a few more red spurts splash onto the ground.

For another half a minute, Piggy's legs twitch, then he becomes still.

Now you know. A murder happened in the yard.

Piggy, your best friend, is dead.

You withdraw to your room and lock the door. You sit on the bed.

Tears pour from your eyes.

Why did mum, dad and the stranger murder your friend?

What have you done to them that they punished you so severely?

Didn't mum and dad know that from the moment you brought him home as a present for dad, Piggy has been your best friend? You took food to him, you stroked him, every other day you tied a rope around his neck and took him for a walk in the woods, where he dug in the ground, looking for truffles. When ripe pears and apples started falling from the trees, you went to the orchard. Piggy gobbled up the fruit with great gusto, particularly the half-rotten ones.

Then the moment came when you stopped being afraid that Piggy would run away, and you let him run around without tying him. He happily stomped around, sniffing and digging here and there; in the woods, he often hid behind trees or bushes. But every time, sooner or later, he was by your side again.

And every time he came back, he rubbed himself against your leg and grunted happily. When you decided to take him home and shut him back in the pigsty that was his home, he followed of his own free will.

He trusted you. He knew you were friends.

He knew nothing bad could happen to him with you.

And now ...

4.

A present for Dad's birthday

Do you remember how Piggy became your friend?
It's all written in your Book of Lists.
Look through and read about it.
Mum said that dad would be celebrating his fortieth birthday and asked you what you were going to buy him. Dad said: 'Leave the boy alone, don't joke with him!'
'And specially not at his expense,' he added.
You've always felt that dad loves you much more than mum. That he has accepted you with all your faults and knows that it's not you who's to blame, but the Unfortunate Event. Mum has never accepted it, perhaps because she carried you inside her for nine months.
Without knowing how and why, you sensed that his fortieth birthday was very important to dad. Mum said it represented half a lifetime.
'That's why you should think about a present for him,' she added.
You could give him a pencil. You've got quite a few. But dad, who works in the municipal offices, has even more. He'd

think you were making fun of him. Birthday presents are usually bought. And you don't have any money. You use up the small change that mum gives you to buy a drink on the way to school and back.

It's true you put a little bit away, just in case, but it's not enough for a present that you wouldn't be ashamed of.

In your anguish, you set off for the next village, Kuželj, to see your granddad Vili, your father's father, where you often go when you didn't know what to do. Granddad is always able to give you advice that most people would say was good or at least the best of all the bad advice available.

Good advice is as rare as hen's teeth, he once told you.

This time, he gave you advice that was not only good, but fantastic. He suggested you give dad a piglet. Being a municipal official, he'd never had anything like that, despite living in the countryside.

A pig is a living being. Pigs are smart, almost as smart as dogs, if not smarter. True, their attitude to hygiene is rather sloppy, but that's part of their nature. You can't imagine a pig showering every day or going to the toilet with a roll of toilet paper in its trotters. That would be possible only in a fairy tale.

But life is not a fairy tale; life is what we live. And life is cruel for many people, perhaps for most people.

For you, too, said granddad.

Piggy will connect dad with nature, with everything that's alive in the world, regardless of its form or mental abilities. There could be no better present for a municipal official.

When you told granddad that you couldn't buy a pig because you didn't have the money and you didn't want to steal one, since stealing wasn't nice and you could end up in prison, where you'd rather not go, granddad stroked your head.

And he said that you didn't have to steal one. He'd also be disappointed if you did so. But you could choose one of the piglets from his pigsties.

He led you behind his house, that stood on a low slope at the edge of the village, and let you peer through the gaps in the ten doors in a line of wooden sheds that he called the pigsties. In each of them you saw ears and eyes and wide pig snouts with bodies of varying sizes behind them.

And almost every pig greeted you with a sound that went approximately like this: 'Gruuuh gruuh, grroh grrroh.'

When you looked into the last one, you saw four little piglets sleeping peacefully, more or less on top of each other. Granddad said that it might happen, in fact it probably would happen, that at first dad would not be happy with his present. But sooner or later he would realise that as well as people and municipal regulations, there were also living beings who prefer something more edible than regulations.

And when after a few months or a year dad realised this, he would grow to love the little pig. And that would make him nicer to you and your mum.

Although that didn't mean that your mum would be nicer to you, he added.

Since you love granddad very much, perhaps more than anyone in the world, for you've never heard an unkind word from him, you saw in his suggestion something that would be good for your dad.

And you said: 'Alright.'

Granddad asked you which piglet you wanted. But at first sight they all looked the same, so you asked him to choose. He said you had to choose yourself. And you pointed at one of the four, the one whose head was resting on another one's tummy. Granddad said you had to give him a name.

'Piggy,' you said. 'He'll be called Piggy.'

5.

Up the hill

Then granddad asked you how you would get Piggy home. And there, he'd have to be shut inside so he wouldn't run away, and he'd need a trough to eat from.
And who would feed him?
You didn't have an answer to any of these questions. You hadn't thought about it at all.
Of course, you could have carried Piggy home, he was still a little piglet and light enough. You'd need twenty minutes, maybe half an hour. But he was smooth and slippery, he could wriggle out of your hands and escape. Maybe into the woods where you wouldn't be able to find him. Perhaps down to the Kolpa, where he might drown.
You looked at granddad. Since he had a solution for every problem, you were sure he'd find a solution for this one, too.
He went to a shed near the pigsty and from the junk inside pulled out a wicker basket, very similar to the one mum kept in the bathroom at home for the dirty washing.

But granddad's basket was so shabby that it probably wasn't for dirty washing.

And it was old, very old.

Granddad said that back in the day when there was no border between Slovenia and Croatia, he used that basket to take apples to the market in Delnice . He had a large orchard and lots of apples. So many, that he took them to the market in Delnice twice a week. But that was in days that were long gone, he said. Now, he was giving you the basket to take the piglet home in.

The basket had shoulder straps. They were shabby and slightly torn, but granddad assured you they were strong enough for you to carry the basket like a rucksack.

The only problem was that the piglet, although little, was heavier than you expected. When granddad put him in the basket and lifted it onto your shoulders, you nearly collapsed. You're small and slight, much smaller than other kids your age.

Besides, the piglet wasn't still, he was throwing himself around, trying to climb out of the basket, which didn't have a lid. Although the basket was too deep for him to do that, his thrashing around would sooner or later have toppled you over and the piglet would jump out and escape.

Again, granddad found a solution.

In front of the house, stood a wooden cart with two wheels and a base at the front that prevented it from tipping over and kept it level. On the cart, were two plastic plant pots. At the front, a stick with a handle was screwed in and if you took the handle, you could pull the cart behind you. Granddad put the plant pots on either side of the front door, lifted the basket with the piglet onto the cart and tied it with a rope to the wooden sides so that it couldn't sway or tip over.

Then he put the handle in your hand and said: 'Now take the piglet home.'

And that's what you did.

You'll never forget Piggy's journey to Laze.

The metal wheels rattled and squeaked noisily on the narrow road. This bothered the piglet more than you, and he kept thrashing around the basket, grunting and making a noise that sounded like crying.

You felt sorry for him. It was obvious he didn't feel comfortable in the basket. When he calmed down for a few moments, you turned and looked around, convinced that he had climbed out onto the road and set off back to granddad's house.

But he stayed in the basket and after a while he didn't move; he'd become resigned to his fate.

Meanwhile, you were getting more and more tired. The summer sun was beating down like mad, and soon you were all sweaty and increasingly afraid that the piglet would die of heat and thirst, especially when you turned left from the main road towards Malenca and then Laze. There, the road went up so steeply that the weight of the cart began to pull you back.

Every thirty steps or so you had to stop and rest, out of breath. You turned the cart sideways so that it wouldn't roll down the hill. During these breaks you looked at the piglet lying curled up at the bottom, breathing fast, and wheezing a little.

For the first time you felt that Piggy was one of the nicest animals in the world. And that, even though you were going to give him to dad for his birthday, he would remain your friend.

Exhausted, you pulled the cart uphill until the road levelled a little. But another steep slope lay ahead, the worst one, so you stopped to gather your strength. Beneath the road a stream ran through a stone tunnel, trickling along the hill beneath the Kuželj rockface and continuing across the meadows on the right to a large stream that came from the left and ran downwards towards the Kolpa.

To the left of the road, there was a hollow in which water gathered, creating a small marsh.

The piglet, probably able to smell the dampness, began to thrash around so hard that the rope tying the basket to the cart became unfastened on one side. The basket tilted, the piglet jumped out and splashed straight into the wet mud on the left. He rolled left and right to freshen up.

Then he started swallowing the mud. You became afraid that he would choke, so you lurched after him and tried to pull him out.

Later it struck you that God himself must have been standing by your side then, for otherwise you would not have managed to hug the wriggling piglet to your chest, climb – covered in mud – back onto the road and throw him into the basket, push it upright again and tie it securely once more to the side of the cart.

Let alone – rather desperately by now – to pull the cart up the last, steepest part of the journey to the old, deserted house and then to the new house, where you collapsed in the yard, exhausted. You lay there for a while, thinking hard where to put the little piglet as you knew that, stinking filthy as he was, he could not be given to dad for his birthday when he got home from work.

The bathroom.

You unlocked the front door, went into the house and opened the bathroom door, which was immediately to the left, went back for the piglet, lifted him out of the basket, carried him inside and put him in the bath. You closed the bathroom door to stop him escaping. But he couldn't climb out of the bath, it was too smooth and his trotters slipped. He couldn't grasp at anything and began squealing again.

You undressed and climbed into the bath. You grabbed the shower head and turned on the tap. And then you showered both of you with cold water. There was so much mud that for a while the drain became blocked. Only when you turned on the hot water did the blockage clear and the dirty water slowly drain away.

And then – you'll never forget this – a connection was established between you. You were kneeling in the bath and the piglet was sitting on his bottom, looking at you.

For a few moments, you stared into each other's eyes.

6.

Dad's stubbornness

Mum, always the first to get home from work, found you in the bath.

She gasped, screamed and ran into the yard. After a while, she came back and asked you what was going on.

You said nothing special: the piglet was your present for dad's fortieth birthday. On the way home, the two of you had fallen into some mud and needed a bath, but now you were clean.

Mum wanted to know where you got the piglet.

You told her.

She said she would take it back immediately. What were you thinking, you dummy? She threw the piglet into the car boot, even though you were crying, begging her not to do it.

The piglet was squealing, he didn't seem to want to go back.

He seemed to want to stay with you.

But just as Mum slammed the boot shut, dad came home. He wanted to know what was happening. 'It's my fortieth birthday. Have you bought the cake for the guests we're expecting tonight?'

'There won't be anyone,' said mum. 'No cake, either. You've got a present that I'm just about to drive back.'

And she opened the car boot in which Piggy lay quietly, letting out his usual, friendly noises.

'Here,' said mum. 'Your son has given you the dirtiest animal in the world for your fortieth. If you want to slaughter it, go ahead, but do it now and I'll do a roast for the guests, if anyone comes, that is. If not, I'll take this filthy thing back and return it to your father, who cooked up the whole idea.'

'Even on your birthday, he's making fun of you,' she added.

'No,' you shouted. 'It's not granddad's fault! It was my idea. Me and the piglet became friends in the bathroom and I'm giving him to dad as a friend for the birthday that signifies half of his life life.'

'You can forget that,' said mum, her face bright red.

But suddenly dad raised his voice.

'It's my right to decide which birthday presents I accept and keep. I won't reject my son's present. What sort of parents are we if we don't allow him to be happy with at least one decision in his life? I've got a pig and I shall keep it.'

Dad didn't rebel against mum often. But he did this time. You felt so relieved.

'And where will you keep it?' said mum in a hoarse voice. 'In the bedroom?'

'I'll think about it,' said dad and lifted Piggy out of mum's car.

'Thanks, son,' he said and looked at you in a similar way to how Piggy had looked at you a bit earlier in the bath. You felt your dad was also your friend.

Dad and Piggy.

But not mum.

Who blamed you for the Unfortunate Event.

Because of snoring.

Dad thought differently. As did everyone else, the teachers, your schoolfriends and even their parents were certain that it wasn't your snoring. Snoring is natural. It's not prohibited by law.

If you snore, you snore.

Some people fart loudly during their sleep. Or scream whilst dreaming. Snoring is nothing to be ashamed of. Farting is worse. Snoring doesn't smell.

And the one who was driven crazy by your snoring constantly farted in his sleep. True, he wasn't aware of it, but you were no more aware of snoring.

These are facts. It's true you haven't come to terms with them, but granddad said that objecting to fact never gets you anywhere.

7.
Piggy acquires a home

Piggy stayed in Laze.

Dad settled him in the empty barn at the old house, which stood by the road just over a hundred metres away and in which no one had lived for a long time.

And you took food to him there, in the empty barn with a door that bolted shut.

Slops. That's what pigs eat, said mum. The leftovers on our plates after breakfast, lunch and dinner. Until then, you had been giving leftovers to the cats that came to the terrace. From then on, you took them to Piggy. He seemed to like them, he even licked the inside of the bowl in which you took him the leftovers.

He also licked dry the water dish. You soon realised that his thirst was greater than his hunger and because you knew that thirst can result in dehydration, which can result in death, you made sure that Piggy's 'apartment' was never without a bucket of water.

Better too much than not enough, you concluded.

In spite of this, after about a month you noticed that Piggy wasn't feeling well. When you sat opposite each other, you saw in his eyes a hint of sadness or maybe of boredom.

Of loneliness?

If not that, then something that was far from happiness and satisfaction.

You were convinced that animals should be happy and satisfied. Especially pigs, who are intelligent and have similar feelings to people.

Without thinking much, you let him out into the open so that he could walk around the orchard. If he escapes, you thought, let him, pigs have a right to freedom, too. You were certain that he would return to granddad's in Kuželj, where he was born.

But Piggy didn't run away. He went over to the house and had a good sniff of everything; he circled the house a few times, sniffed all the trees in the orchard, each and every one. In between, he dug up a few things you couldn't recognise because of the distance, and ate them, and then he ran up and down the road a few times, as if training for a pig marathon.

At last he stopped at the top of the hill, where the road began to descend to Kuželj. There he sat for a long time, looking at the valley. You thought he was remembering his life at granddad's. And that he wanted to go back.

But no, after a while, he returned to the abandoned barn in the old house and went to sleep.

You realised he would not run away.

And why would he?

You'd become friends, hadn't you?

You started going on walks together. Around the orchard, the fields, the neighbours' orchards and fields, the woods, all the way down to the Kolpa and along its bank. A few times

Piggy even joined you in the shallow water by the river's edge. And twice, not just once but twice, he waited for you in the middle of the woods at the top of the hill where you took a shortcut to your school in Fara or back home, when you didn't feel like waiting for the bus.

As if he knew when you would be coming home from school.

And what did he do when he spotted you on the path between the trees? He stood there, wagging his tail and grunting.

Dad soon lost interest in Piggy. You didn't hold that against him, he had a demanding job. And he had a wife, your mum, who did everything to get on your nerves as much as possible.

Then granddad came by one day. He was brought by his neighbour in his old car. Mum and dad were at work, but you hadn't gone to school. You knew that you would give a headache as a reason, your usual excuse. You'd long ago stopped feeling guilty for making up excuses. Good job you'd stayed at home, otherwise you'd have missed granddad's visit!

Granddad and his neighbour took some planks of wood, painted black, out of the car boot. Granddad measured twenty steps from the house to the edge of the yard, where the orchard began. He drew a square in the soil. And on this square, using nails and hammers, granddad and his neighbour constructed a large crate from the wood which, after they had finished, granddad called a pigsty.

Let Piggy be nearer the house. The barn in the old house was too big, pigs prefer smaller spaces, they get bored and start feeling lonely. And it was too far for you to carry food to. Let Piggy, like all pigs in the world, have a pigsty.

And then granddad and his neighbour brought Piggy from the barn at the old house to his new home. You didn't object.

You were happy. Now you could see Piggy's home through the window. You could hear him grunt. You could go out and talk to him.

What a shame, you often thought, that you couldn't talk to Piggy in your language.

But it was enough to be able to talk in his.

You learned to grunt.

8.

A present for your birthday

Look through the window and return to the present.
What's happening in the yard?
The morning is fully awake. Although the sun is still behind the hills, the light is clear enough so that you can't explain what you're seeing as an extended nightmare.
Your friend Piggy is lying on two wide planks of wood, placed on two trestles. His legs are sticking up into the air whilst your dad and the stranger with a sharp knife are skinning him.
They're doing this silently and meticulously, slightly bent over, focused on their work. As if performing an operation on a live person. Bit by bit, they are cutting Piggy's skin off, revealing the white fat that resembles lard, which mum often buys in the shop.
Mum isn't there anymore, she took the bowl with Piggy's blood into the house.
You really want to move away from the window and not just away from the window but leave the house completely,

to escape into the woods, find refuge in the darkest, densest part, where no one will hear you cry, scream and howl.

But you can't.

You're numb. Even your little fingers are numb. You'd like to wipe the tears trickling into your mouth, but you can't lift your hand.

You can't even close your eyes.

When the skin has been removed, arranged like a small carpet and placed on top of a stack of firewood nearby, dad and the stranger use their knives to cut up your friend.

Mum has just come out of the house with three large bowls. Two are metal and one plastic. She puts them all on the ground and goes back in. The two butchers (you can't believe one of them is your dad) are chucking pieces of Piggy's dead body into the bowls. Legs into one, intestines that your dad and his assistant lift out of the stomach together splash into the large bucket, whilst into the third bowl go the kidneys and liver. And stomach. And heart.

Don't close your eyes, look through the window.

Face up to what's happening to your friend. Learn the true nature of the world you live in.

When your friend's heart plops into the bowl, you black out.

Faint.

As you sink into darkness, you're certain you are dying.

Then, it's hard to say how many minutes or hours later, you find yourself once more in the world that you will also leave one day.

You feel sorry that you haven't left it already.

You're sitting at the kitchen table. Mum pulls out of the oven a wide pan, in which she has roasted something dark red. Like a big pancake, about a centimetre and a half thick.

She puts the pan on the table.

She cuts off a piece of the dark red thing and puts it on your plate.

'A special present for your fifteenth birthday,' she says with a generous smile.

You want to know what's in the pan.

'Something we don't eat every day,' says mum. 'A rare treat.'

'For really special occasions,' she adds.

You give in and taste it.

It doesn't seem bad. Rather salty, with some pepper. Perhaps there's an egg in there as well. Or maybe not. Because the flavour is something special; something you don't recognise. Something you've never eaten before.

'Eat up,' says mum encouragingly. 'It's all for you.'

And you eat. You're numb, you can't think.

Meanwhile, the butcher and dad are bringing into the kitchen the bowls with the parts of your Piggy. Liver, lungs, stomach, kidneys, trotters. And then the haunches that dad says will make nice smoked leg of pork that you've always liked. He will turn the rest into minced lard and pork sausages.

You'll be eating Piggy for a whole year.

You swallow the last bit of the tasty pancake.

'Although,' says dad, 'no part of a pig is better than the freshly roasted blood that you've just finished off.'

The world spins around you.

You sink into darkness.

9.

Questions without answers

Look through the window.
The sun is shining, it's a beautiful Sunday. You feel like going into the woods.
Then you remember.
For your birthday, your parents slaughtered your best friend, Piggy. And roasted his blood for you. And you ate it.
You rush down the stairs.
And through the open front door towards the orchard.
And you run. Not towards the woods, but to the valley. To granddad's. Your face is wet with tears. You wish you could die.
How will you live without your friend?
Granddad is sitting on his wicker armchair in front of the door, reading the Sunday paper. You ran so fast that you're out of breath and you collapse in a heap in front of him.
Granddad helps you up. He plants you in the armchair. He goes into the house and returns with a wooden chair. He sits on it, leans forward and looks at you.

'Granddad,' you croak.

'What is it?' he says and waits patiently for you to gather yourself.

And you tell him.

The whole story. From the moment in the early morning when you saw the stranger. You thought it was a refugee. That he was hungry. That he would break into the house and kill you all and eat you all. And then move into the house. Or burn it down and move on to Austria.

But it wasn't a refugee.

It was a Butcher. A killer of animals.

Something terrible happened. You don't know what to do. You want revenge. On the way to Kuželj, you vomited up Piggy's blood. But only from your stomach. It has made its way to your very heart and you can't remove it from there.

You'll have to live with the blood of your murdered friend in your heart.

'Can I move in with you?' you ask.

Granddad looks at you and says nothing. There is so much warmth in his eyes.

And sadness.

He is confused and doesn't know what to say.

'But ...' he begins and stops. 'Why do you think we raise pigs? So that we can slaughter them, cut them up and eat them.'

'But not the meat of your best friend!' you shout.

'And not as a birthday present' you add.

'But the pig was a birthday present' says granddad. 'To your father. You gave the pig to him.'

You can't deny that's how it was. But then, you tell granddad, Piggy became your friend. You walked together through the orchard, the woods. You sat together on the slope above the house and watched the sunset. You comforted him when there was a storm and he squealed because he was afraid of the thunder.

'Did you tell your mum and dad this?' granddad asks.

You admit that you didn't.

You were convinced they understood what was happening. After all, you spent most of your free time with Piggy. How could they not know that Piggy was your only friend?

Since you didn't have any others.

'Poor lad,' say granddad.

'I'll drown myself in the Kolpa,' you say.

You get up, as if to run towards the river.

But granddad's hand, surprisingly strong for his years, stops you. He pushes you back into the wicker chair.

'Listen,' he says.

Then suddenly, he doesn't know how to continue.

Nor do you. It seems everything nice is over.

'Come with me,' says granddad.

You go with him behind the house to the pigsties, to the cells in which the pigs that are condemned to death are kept. Some are young, some older, enormous, fat. As you get closer, they start to make their usual noise. You never knew how to describe the noise that was neither grunting nor squealing, but which sounded more like a greeting. Something that expressed pleasure to see you. Perhaps the hope for food.

'Will you kill all of them?' you ask.

'Just one,' he says with a nod. 'When winter comes. I'll sell the others. That's what I live off, my dear grandson. That's why I raise them. My pension isn't enough.'

'Which one will you kill?'

'The first in line. Or the last one left when I've sold the others. That's how it will probably be. Buyers come in late autumn. I'll save one to make sausages and other things for the winter.'

'Will you roast and eat his blood?'

'Of course,' says granddad. 'You get it in blood sausage, as well. I'm sure you must have eaten it.'

You remember that you have.

Often.

You turn around to run off, but again granddad's hand stops you.

'Wait,' he says.

And he explains to you, slowly and with emphasis, in the hope that in your despair you won't miss anything about how the world into which you were born works, the world where you have to fight for survival like all the rest.

Everything that lives needs food. Even plants and flowers and grass need water. And sunlight. And the minerals they get with water. And of course, some animals must eat other animals for food. And men must eat plants *and* animals. That's how it has always been. If we didn't kill and eat animals, we would have disappeared off the face of the earth long ago. Maybe we have gone too far and maybe there are too many people and this will backfire on us.

But for now, that's how things are. And don't think that it's any different in the sea. The big fish eat the little ones.

Your Piggy is no more. You need to accept that.

'But pigs suffer,' you say. 'They're locked up. Sentenced to death.'

'Oh,' says granddad dejectedly. 'If you want, I can give you another pig. And you'll have a friend again.'

'But you'll slaughter that one, as well!'

'Would you rather he died slowly and in pain, from old age? As I will soon? And everyone in the world? Talk to your mum and dad. They don't know everything, they don't know a lot, but they do have more experience than you. And they understand a lot. Including you. Never think that you understand yourself better than others do.'

Pavla, you think. Miss Pavla, the school librarian. She's the only one who can give you some real advice.

You free yourself from granddad's hand and run towards Vas. The village of Vas is just before Fara, where your school is. That's where Miss Pavla lives. But it's the holidays, the height of summer, maybe she's not at home. Maybe she went to the seaside, she deserves a holiday as well.

But you still try.

You run along the narrow road through the wood towards Gladloka and then onwards, until you get to Grivac, and then on towards Petrina, where there's a border crossing and you can go across the bridge over the Kolpa to Croatia. You're all sweaty and so tired that you might collapse at any moment. But you don't stop.

You must get to Miss Pavla's.

Soon after you leave Grivac, a police car pulls up beside you, one of those that drives up and down all the time on the lookout for refugees crossing the Kolpa.

'Where are you hurrying to?' asks the friendly young police officer behind the wheel. Next to him is a woman police officer.

Out of breath, you explain that you must get to Miss Pavla's, the school librarian, who lives in Vas, because you have to ask her something. You live in Laze beneath Kuželj, you explain, and go to school in Fara. Miss Pavla lends you books and now you have to ask her something urgently.

The police officers ask you to get in.

After a short drive, they drop you in Vas.

But Miss Pavla is not at home. You knock on the door of her modest house, but there's no answer. You're disappointed, almost in despair.

You return over the hills and through the woods to Laze.

It takes a long time. When you get home, night is falling. When you're next to the old house you see that mum, dad and granddad are sitting on the porch and that he is telling them something. Mum and dad look downcast. Then granddad gets up to go back to Kuželj. You hide behind the corner of the old house so that he doesn't see you. Mum and dad go inside. You run to the door, open it quietly and with the last of your strength climb the stairs and lock yourself in your room.

After a short while, someone knocks on your door.

'We're sorry,' says mum. 'We didn't know.'

Just when you think she's already gone back downstairs, she speaks again.

'We wanted to make you happy.'

And then, after some moments: 'I know there's many things you can't understand. But you could at least understand this – that we love you.'

10.

Who's the smartest?

Look through the window.

Mum and dad are at work. You're at home alone. You can watch television, you can Google things. You're glad you have the internet, although due to the bad connection it doesn't always work.

But now it is working.

Use it. Try to find out as much as you can about pigs.

While yours was still alive, the others didn't interest you. You knew they were more intelligent than dogs. And that was enough. After talking to granddad, you became concerned about the fate of all the pigs in the world. There must be thousands of them, you think, maybe millions. And they are all locked up. In such a small space that they can't turn round. And all waiting for someone with a knife to come for them.

You're surprised this didn't interest you before.

You're even more amazed at the information you find online.

You make a list. One of the many in your Book of Lists.
Google tells you that pigs really are smarter than dogs, but they're not the smartest.
The smartest animals are apes and monkeys. Chimpanzees, gorillas, orangutans, baboons, macaques.
And then whales, dolphins, elephants.
Pigs are only in tenth place.
Dogs aren't even mentioned
You keep searching and find other lists.
On one, rats are in fifth place, crows in sixth.
Then dogs and pigeons.
Pigs are only ninth.
Who roll in mud, not because they want to be dirty ('dirty pig', says mum), but because they have no sweat glands and the mud cools them.
And right behind pigs – octopuses!
Who have 130 million neurones in their brains. Although most of their neurones are not in their brain, but in their tentacles, each of which has its own intelligence.
A tentacle that is cut off can swim on its own and wrap itself around prey, just like before, but it can't eat it.
The octopus quickly grows a new one.
Isn't it a shame that people, who are the most intelligent among living beings, at least some of them are, do not have similar capabilities?
Because then you could grow a brand new, undamaged brain!
But admit it: in spite of the Unfortunate Event, you still have enough brain.
Considerably less than before, that's true. You lost the capabilities that even your most stupid peers have. But some others were strengthened.
Very much so!

The only pity is that you had no choice. If you had, you'd rather have kept all the capabilities you had before the Unfortunate Event.

Especially memory.

To remember absolutely every little thing. To become a kind of walking Google, so that you never had to search for things to find out what you once knew.

But above all, you'd like to be the kind of Google that had only correct data about things.

Not a hundred different ones.

Keep searching.

Opinions about which animal is the smartest couldn't differ more. That chimpanzees are the smartest seems likely to you, or at least most of the experts agree about that. After all, we have 98 per cent of our genes in common. Because of that two per cent, we are people rather than apes. Chimpanzees make and use simple tools, hunt in groups, often fight amongst themselves, and are violent and cruel.

The last quality in particular connects them most strongly with man.

There is no agreement online about how intelligent dolphins are, if at all. It's true they use a kind of sponge to protect their snouts when they are looking for food on the ocean floor and there is plenty of evidence that they communicate with each other using strange noises, and they can be taught to do tricks in captivity, but that still leaves them a long way behind people.

Elephants are much closer to us and not just because of the size of their brain. They are capable of comforting a member of their family, even helping other animals in difficulty, they communicate with each other through creating vibrations in the ground with their feet.

And what's more: they can recognise themselves in a mirror.

Recognising yourself is the most reliable sign of intelligence.

You are very surprised about how intelligent crows are. You'd never have thought that they knew how to use tools. They make tools from twigs, feathers and other things to help them get to otherwise unreachable bits of food. One crow was observed bending a piece of wire into a hook with its beak to extract a piece of bread from a narrow glass tube.

Google teaches you what you knew before the Unfortunate Event: that among all the millions of animal species of in the world, there isn't one that doesn't try to survive.

And lives in order to find food while trying to avoid becoming food for some other animal. Isn't the beetle that can change its appearance in a moment so that it looks like the bark of the tree on which it is sitting intelligent?

In spite of all the data you find on the internet, you don't stop believing that pigs are the most intelligent creatures in the world. Haven't scientists shown that they can use their snout to move the cursor on a computer screen? That they can tell the difference between images they have already seen and those they haven't? It's possible to train them like dogs, some smaller breeds are kept as house pets, in many places they are used for hunting truffles.

You and Piggy had also looked for them when walking in the woods.

Because their bodies closely resemble the structure of the human body, scientists use them to research inherited diseases. They are also incredibly useful as a source of insulin for treating diabetes. The day is not far off, you find on Google, when a pig's internal organs – kidneys, liver and lungs, perhaps even the heart – will be transplanted to human patients.

There is more than enough evidence that we don't raise pigs only to eat them.

How is it possible that mum and dad don't know that? That they didn't notice the friendship between you and Piggy?

11.

Goodbye to the world?

Since the Unfortunate Event you've had a speech defect. You sometimes stammer and leave long pauses in sentences when you're looking for the right word, so you decide to write your parents a letter. By hand on an A4 sheet of paper.

Like in the old days. You won't use the computer, because everyone does that now. In any case, you don't even know their email addresses, they've never told you.

Maybe they don't even have email addresses.

'Dear mum, dear dad,' you write. 'You killed my friend Piggy and forced me to eat his blood. You have killed the creature that is dearest in the world to me. And my Piggy was a good pig, very, very good. Even if he went into the wood on his own, he always came back and pressed his snout against my leg. Why? Because he was happy to see me. Of course, he's not the only pig who had to die a violent death. People kill 24 million of them every week for sausages and hams and liver and kidneys and lard. Every week! Can you imagine if every week 24 million people were killed and turned into sausages.

I know that you two are not interested in that. I've noticed that few things interest you. And those that do interest you, don't interest you very much. You stopped talking to me like we used to talk before the Unfortunate Event. Maybe it's the fault of the time we live in. That's what Miss Pavla the school librarian says, who is, besides Piggy, my only friend. Everything is the fault of the time we live in, she says. Miss Pavla knows and understands. She spends most of her time among books and reads a lot, because things interest her. What interests you, mum and dad?

I can't describe how bad I feel after your murder of my friend Piggy. I no longer feel at home with you. Maybe I'll go away, although I don't know where. Maybe into the unknown, maybe to another world. Parents who kill their children's friends would be telling a terrible lie if they said they loved their children. I'd like to forgive you your crime, but I don't know if I can. Maybe one day I will wake up and find with relief that I am dead.'

You fold the letter and put it in the Book of Lists, which you hide beneath the bed. For now, you don't know what you will do with it.

Maybe you won't even give it to mum and dad.

But the main thing is, you've clarified some things to yourself.

Look through the window.

See the trees, the flowers, the wood, listen to the birds, listen to the animals in the woods behind the hill, the cries and groans, so that you don't know whether it is a roe buck, a bear or a fox. Turn to the right, towards the Kolpa, to Kuželj and to the wooded hills on the other side of the river, which are in Croatia, look up at the sky, where peaceful white clouds are placidly sailing.

You live in one of the most beautiful places in Europe. You are safe, nothing threatens you. Why would you like to leave this world?

Yes, your soul is wounded. And it hurts.

But look through the window and allow your eyes to soak up all the beauty spread out beneath you. There won't be this on the other side.

If you think it will be nice on the other side, you're mistaken.

On the other side, there'll be nothing. And you won't even know.

Just like your Piggy doesn't know that he is no longer.

For some time, he'll be present on this side in the form of leg of pork, sausages and minced lard, which your mum will put on bread for you before you go to school each morning. He'll still be your friend. And the more of him you eat and with the greater enjoyment, the deeper will be your friendship.

Your dad spent a lot of time convincing you of that. And he really did try, considering that he rarely speaks more than three words together.

Why don't you want to believe him?

Because he doesn't understand that you suffered an injustice. And you don't like injustices. Even when they happen to other people. You don't even like injustices when they happen to people who you dislike. And everything that happens around the world, everything you see on the television, all those injustices, great and small, bad and worse.

But the injustice that you suffered is the worst of them all.

Perhaps even worse than the one that damaged your brain. That was done in anger. The murder of your friend Piggy was carefully planned, in secret, behind your back.

Every injustice has consequences.

The consequence of this injustice can only be your withdrawal from the world.

Not because you hate your mum and dad. You're not capable of that. After all, they worry about you. And not because you're angry with them.

The only feelings you can find inside you since the Unfortunate Event are fear, anxiety and disappointment.

You no longer feel joy, or happiness.

And so, your decision to depart the world is irreversible.

12.

The Book of Lists

Look through the window.

There, beneath the pear tree, where you and Piggy often sat and talked. You talked and Piggy listened. He got used to sitting on his bottom, like a dog. You often put your arm around his neck. You sat close together and stared at the valley. And at the sky. And at the wooded hills on the other side of the Kolpa. It seemed that he understood what you were saying.

His smell didn't bother you. In fact, you liked it.

You explained to him that all of life is made up of lists. Lists of things and events. And you wrote things in a special book that you always had with you, so that you could check whether you'd forgotten.

And since the Unfortunate Event, you forget most things

Life is a long list of events, you explained to Piggy. You slip in the bathtub, hit your head, an event. Mum and dad exchange some unpleasant words, an event. You come back from school with flu, an event. A schoolmate calls you a 'dummy', an event.

And so on.

Almost every hour, something happens that is an event.

When you connect events, you get a story. You can connect them in different ways and get different stories. Depending on how you connect lists of events, your life appears in a hundred different ways. And you get the feeling that you are living a hundred lives at once.

That fills you with anxiety.

And so, you don't often connect lists of events into bigger lists, or small stories into bigger ones. Although you sometimes feel like doing so. And in the end, get to the story that you could call 'the story of my life'.

You're afraid you wouldn't like it.

And so, you stay with individual stories. You don't connect the lists into a complete list, which would show you as you may not really be.

Maybe it only seemed to you that Piggy understood what you were saying. Maybe he didn't understand a single word. He was just happy that you were talking to him. He felt that you valued him.

He, too, was happy that he had a friend.

So, you sat on the grass beneath the pear tree almost every other day and sometimes at night. You told him that you started the Book of Lists before the Unfortunate Event. And that the 'before' lists were different from the 'after' ones.

The lists before the Unfortunate Event included, among other things, plans for your future career. You intended to be a military pilot, the captain of a submarine, an inventor, a computer programmer, the director of a multinational company, a doctor, a nursery school teacher, the General Secretary of the United Nations, a secret agent, an astronaut. A footballer.

You knew that you couldn't be all at once, but the endless possibilities gave you the feeling that the world was a nice place.

And that you would become someone in it

You also wrote in the book a list of the girls at school that you liked. You didn't list the most beautiful ones, but the cleverest. If possible, even cleverer and better than you in at least one subject. Among them were three who were also among the most beautiful. They had no advantage because of that; they were on the list because of their intellectual abilities.

Because you were by far the best pupil in the class, the list wasn't long. On it were Marinka, Jana, Katja, Barbara, Gabriela, Mili and Sandra. No one else deserved to be on the list.

You had already decided back then that you would marry one of them when the time came. Although it didn't seem as if that would really happen, because none of the listed girls showed any particular interest in you. You were the best pupil in the class and one of the best in the school, but you weren't particularly good looking.

You weren't ugly, far from it, but you had slightly irregular features, your nose was too big, you had a receding chin and sticking out ears. And though you were of average height, your legs were too short for your body. Your chosen ones, even the cleverest, preferred sporty types with regular features, even if they had low grades.

You did have some friends among the chosen ones, but as soon as you dropped a hint to one or other of them that you liked her, then they began to avoid you.

That slowly caused a wound in your heart. Because you were gifted, you were convinced that you were entitled to everything in life. When you realised it was not so, you decided to exclude girls from your mind and to get interested in them again in a good five years' time, when they would be grown up and they would realise that looks are not the most important thing in the world.

At the end of the day, your mum and dad were not the best-looking people in the world, far from it. But they still got married and made you.
And were proud of you.
Until the Unfortunate Event. And then no more.
You understood that your mum's dreams had also been destroyed. It meant a lot to her that she had a son who would go to grammar school, who would study something complicated, do an important job, win a number of awards, be respected everywhere he went, even outside Slovenia. She also enjoyed praising her son's success. And then suddenly: the dream was over.
No grammar school, no university, no career.
Cruel?
It was a good job that after the Unfortunate Event, your feelings were also dulled.
Your Book of Lists became different. You wrote in it things that before the Unfortunate Event you kept in your head and connected in a different way. And they had a different meaning. You knew that there was now something wrong with you. But at the same time, you felt that what was wrong with you was not *very* wrong, not *terribly* wrong.
You were still you.
And you acquired a skill that you didn't have before: learning foreign languages, just like that. Although all the experts said that this ability was in truth 'autistic', however useful it may seem, but you didn't care what others thought. You were satisfied that you learned English and German almost in passing, mainly from the internet and watching television.
And when someone suggested that, considering you couldn't go to grammar school, that you should learn Arabic and get a fully-paid job as an official interpreter on the border that so many refugees were crossing, which for someone aged fifteen

would have been an exceptional achievement, you said stubbornly: 'Two foreign languages are enough.'

You regretted everything that the Unfortunate Event had taken away from you.

The feeling of joy that you were alive, and that the future was before you.

The feeling of hope that one of the clever girls at school would take an interest in you.

The physical skill and flexibility that you proudly displayed at PE. After the Unfortunate Event, your movements were awkward, and clumsy.

Your talent for maths, at which you simply shone. Now you even had problems adding up.

Your computer skills and the hope that one day you would hack into the systems of the governments of the biggest countries in the world, and manipulate them to ensure world peace. Now you mastered only surfing the internet, and looking for the information that you once possessed.

But most of all, you regretted the friends that once fought for your attention: since the Unfortunate Event they were ashamed to hang out with you.

You told all this to Piggy during one of your talks, when you were sitting beneath the pear tree, looking at the valley.

At night, you and Piggy observed the moon above the hill and admired its beauty. You told Piggy you regretted that you were born too late to be among the first to step on its surface. Maybe you'd be the first to set foot on Mars.

But after the Unfortunate Event, that was no longer possible.

Piggy gave a quiet grunt.

It seemed that he was agreeing with you.

13.

How to kill yourself

You are suddenly aware of a decision to leave this world, which is without your friend Piggy.
How will you do it?
Look through the window.
Above you, high into the sky, rises the frightening Kuželj rockface. A high, rocky outcrop with a flat top and a steep, almost vertical fall. You could climb up, go to the edge on the left and hurl yourself off. You would be smashed against the rocks at the foot and all your thoughts would be extinguished in a second.
Or not.
For the rockface is not straight and vertical, but in places slightly at an angle and serrated, while at the foot it widens into rocky disorder with hollows and sharp edges. You could break every bone in your body, shred all your soft tissue, but you might not die.
You would live on for many years, in a wheelchair, in great pain.

Forget about rocks.

In films on the television you have seen endless suicide attempts, some successful, some less so. Most often, people cut their wrists. With a razor blade or a knife. Like the one you keep hidden beneath the bed, for example, in case one of the monsters you dream about should come through the window. First your left arm, then your right. And you would bleed out. You would turn on the bath tap. Fill it with water, get in, cut your wrists and watch how the water darkened, changed into blood, how the life ebbed from you, how you were slowly embraced by peace and silence. On the edge of the bathtub, you would stick a message: 'Mum, a present for your birthday. Please roast my blood and eat it.'

You know that would be too harsh a punishment for her.

You begin to think of other ways of disembarking from the ship of life.

Particularly quick and painless ones.

Jumping off a high bridge could be like that. But the distance between the bridge and the water beneath it must be great enough, so that when you hit the water, you would not only be hurt and realise that you were still alive, but that you immediately lost consciousness and drowned. For such a death, the most appropriate bridge, perhaps even the only appropriate one, is the Golden Gate Bridge in San Francisco, which is, you've heard on the television, a real magnet for suicides.

But San Francisco is far away. Too far.

What else is there?

Tablets. Mum has trouble sleeping and so every evening when she goes to bed, she takes a white tablet that she removes from a plastic bottle. She keeps the tablets in the drawer of her bedside cabinet.

Go and have a look.

You open the drawer and find there are only three tablets in there. Too few to send you to sleep forever. The doctor is sure to have prescribed her some new ones, but she probably keeps them in her handbag or maybe she hasn't picked them up yet from the chemist. You could wait, but it could take several days, and during that time you might have second thoughts.

You must act before that.

Many people in films kill themselves by putting a gun in their mouth and blowing their brains out. Death is instantaneous, you checked on Google. If not death, at least unconsciousness. And because it happens in a moment, you feel no pain.

But where to get a gun?

You don't know anyone who has one.

And what if you did know someone? What reason could you give for wanting to borrow it?

It seems that it's impossible to depart this world without pain.

Then you remember the Kolpa, with the exception of Piggy, your best friend. Regardless of how cold the water is, you go there to bathe, not only in the summer, but also the spring and late autumn. Everyone is amazed that you like such cold water. Mum and dad have told you many times that you're not allowed to bathe in the river.

Except in the summer, when it is not so cold, and they sometimes even brave it themselves.

But you like icy water. After the initial shock, your body comes awake, your memory is refreshed, your mind is clearer, you are aware of things that normally slip past you. So, you like going to bathe in the icy Kolpa. You go there to wake up, to forge a link with yourself as you were before the Unfortunate Event.

Why not go to sleep in the river where you go to wake up? Although there's no doubt that drowning can be unpleasant.

You Google it and get some frightening information.

Beneath the water, you will instinctively try to hold your breath as long as you can, so that water does not force its way into your windpipe and lungs. You will be gripped by panic, in an instinctive fight for survival, you will begin to thrash around, which will reduce the amount of oxygen in your blood and shorten the time it takes to pass out. You will try to cough out the water from your windpipe, or to swallow it, which means that even more water will force its way in.

It will take a quite a while for you to lose consciousness. You'll try to get to the surface to breathe. However firm your decision, you will try to save yourself.

It won't be pleasant, far from it.

Should you wait for a natural death? In sixty or seventy years? To the end of the century?

Without Piggy, without other friends, without your parents, who understand you?

You don't wish for such a fate.

In spite of your reservations, drowning in the Kolpa seems like the most suitable way to bid goodbye to the world.

Not only because it will be an old friend sucking you under, but because it will quickly carry your body to the River Sava, which flows into the Danube, which flows into the Black Sea. And so, after death you'll experience the journey to distant lands that has always been one of your greatest wishes.

14.

Some are fated to die sad

Look through the window.

The sun is shining on the orchard. In the shadow of the tree where you first saw Piggy's Killer, mum and dad are sitting, each in their wicker chair, several metres apart. Dad is reading the paper, mum a magazine. As usual.

It's Sunday

Like the day when they killed Piggy.

Sundays are bad days.

It seems that there is tension between mum and dad.

There are so many things that they have done wrong.

They disappointed you most with the decision to move from Kočevje to Laze, in the back of beyond, where they had built a weekend house for their retirement. This house has an upstairs and six rooms altogether and is much bigger than the small flat in Kočevje, which they rent out to supplement their income. Their salaries aren't very high, but not so low that they can't afford summer holidays. So, you have spent some weekends abroad: in London, Paris, Venice, even Istanbul.

And, of course, every summer, ten days on the Croatian coast.

When the house was built, they said there was no sense in waiting for retirement, they could move to the village straight away, they could drive to work, there was an orchard there, a big garden where they could grow vegetables, two fields, a small area of woodland, enough for firewood, and a hundred metres away an old, abandoned house that had belonged to mum's parents, who are now dead.

And down below in Kuželj, beside the road, lived granddad, dad's father, who could help with jobs at home, although he would soon need help himself.

It sounded nice.

The only problem was, they didn't ask you what you thought.

It didn't seem to them important that you had schoolfriends in Kočevje, who you would miss. That you'd have to go to school in Fara, where you didn't know anyone, and the other kids may not like you. That you'd have to go quite far to school, with a school bus that came at six every morning and after school brought you back to Osilnica.

Sometimes the bus is late, which means that you have to wait in Fara the whole afternoon or walk home across the hills and through the woods, where you might meet a bear.

Mum and dad always thought mainly of themselves.

Do they love each other? Like other mums and dads love each other?

And why did they only have you? Why did you never get a little brother or sister? How different your life would be if you weren't alone!

Or maybe not.

Maybe you'd be lonely then, as well, like you've been for a long time, with a strange emptiness in your heart, like now, which seems to you to be getting bigger and bigger, and you don't know what causes it.

'It is the fate of some to live and die in sadness,' Miss Pavla said to you once.

You realised then that Miss Pavla is also alone and lonely. She also feels an emptiness inside. But when you were together in the school library and talked, it was as if a sticking plaster had been placed over a raw wound in your souls.

However, all that is no longer important.

You have decided to drown yourself.

Look through the window.

Mum and dad are still reading, and they still haven't spoken a word.

You realise once more that they are not particularly good looking. In fact, you've known this for a long time, ever since the moment when you realised that you yourself are not. Perhaps you might have been, if you'd had better looking parents.

'Don't let it bother you,' said Miss Pavla once. 'Some are good looking, some are clever. There are very few who are both. Be glad that you're clever.'

If your mum and dad hadn't murdered your friend Piggy, you might still have become something in life.

But now it's too late.

You've made up your mind.

Will they miss you?

If the rivers carry you to the Black Sea, you might get washed ashore in Istanbul, and you'd happily send them a postcard.

What would you write on it? Probably nothing.

Or maybe you'd draw Piggy on it.

But none of that is possible.

When you're dead, you're Nothing, don't delude yourself about that.

You take the Book of Lists, you don't want to leave it for them to see, let it drown with you, and you quietly go downstairs.

To the road towards Kuželj.

'Where are you going?' mum calls after you.

'To granddad's,' you lie.

15.

First liberation action

When you come to the road beneath the hill, a police van is driving from the direction of Osilnica. A male police officer is driving and a female officer is in the passenger seat.

On the back seats are three young men with dark skin, an older man and two children, a boy and a girl. Evidently the police caught them when they came across the Kolpa from the Croatian side.

Refugees.

Where are they from? Where are they taking them? What will become of them?

The police van drives towards Petrina, while you carry on along the grassy path towards the trees on the riverbank.

Then you remember granddad, who lives in Kuželj, ten minutes' walk along the road towards Osilnica.

Wouldn't it be right to say goodbye to him?

He has always been kind to you. He's never harmed you in any way. He gave you the piglet that became Piggy, your best friend.

Wouldn't you like to squeeze his hand before you depart for the other world? Of course, you won't tell him what you're planning. You could say it's Sunday, so you came to visit.

You go back to the road and head for Kuželj.

But granddad is not at home.

Did he go to mass in Fara?

Probably. It's the right time. It has never bothered you that granddad goes to mass and gets worked up because your mum and dad never go, since they are convinced that religion brings nothing good to the world and will only contribute to the fact that it will soon be over.

You value granddad's loyalty to his faith. And his belief in God. You've often asked him to explain what it all means.

At times, it seems to you that God is what you're most missing in your life.

But it's too late now.

If God exists, you're sure to meet him on the other side. You're convinced that he won't hide his face from you. You've never offended him, you've never done anything that might be labelled a sin.

Because granddad's not at home, you decide at least to say goodbye to his pigs.

You go behind the house and towards the pigsties. The pigs sense your approach and begin to grunt excitedly. Not from fear, but in the hope that you've brought them some food.

Pigs are always hungry, you've known that a long time.

And unhappy in the wooden crates, in which they can't even turn around.

Rescue them. Set them free, onto the meadow, into the wood, where they'll look for truffles.

Just like Piggy did.

Why do people demand freedom for themselves and not for pigs and other animals?

You can find no answer to that question. You just know that granddad's pigs would feel better in the meadows or the woods than in the crates.

And you let them out.

They are amazed when they realise that they can move without hitting against anything. The squeal and grunt and let out all the other pig noises, including those that you know no word for. But it seems to you that they are happy, because they've been rescued from their own filth, which granddad has evidently not cleaned up for some days.

There are seven of them, four big, three little ones. Roughly the same size as Piggy when you got him as a gift.

They sniff around, try to eat some grass, which they don't like, and then they go on to the road and towards the village. They are following the biggest of them, which you quickly notice is a sow, for there are three young ones constantly hanging off her swollen teats,

They come to the bridge that leads across the Kolpa to Croatian Kuželj. On Sundays the place is empty, no one to be seen.

When they get to the middle of the bridge, they stop for a moment and look back towards the Slovene side. And then the sow leads them forward to the other side.

Refugees, you think.

Refugees going in the opposite direction, with no idea of where they will end up.

16.

Underwater

You go back to the grassy path that leads to the bank of the Kolpa. You turn right, walking slowly across the soft grass. You take off your sandals so that you can feel it. So that you can feel, while it is still possible, the ground beneath your feet. The feeling is a pleasant one, it connects you to this world that you will soon no longer be conscious of.

You are overcome by doubts.

Is your decision really firm enough? Will you persist to the end? Would it be better to wait a little?

What if mum and dad really did see their cruel action as a present for your birthday?

You could get revenge by going around Slovenia, liberating suffering pigs from the crowded pig farms – pigs who had nothing to look forward to other than slaughter.

But no, these are just excuses, because you're becoming scared. The closer you get to the river, the clearer it becomes to you that drowning will not be pleasant. But you see no way back. You couldn't live with the thought that not only are you a 'dummy', but also a coward.

You'd be ashamed for the rest of your life.

When you get to the trees beside the river, you see that the water level is low because it hasn't rained for a long time, and it's foaming and leaping when it hits against the protruding rocks, sharp and serrated, right across to the Croatian side. You could certainly find a spot where the water is deep enough to drown in, but you doubt that the current would carry you to the Sava and the Danube and the Black Sea.

Whatever. You begin to undress, as you always do before you wade into the water to get to the depth where you can start swimming.

But why, you ask yourself. This time, you're not going swimming. Your clothes will be found on the bank, they will be identified, and your mum and dad will know what you have done. You would like to disappear in such a way that they would never find out what became of you.

You'll have to drown with your clothes on.

What about the Book of Lists? Do you really want it to drown with you? That every trace of the 'dummy' – who before the Unfortunate Event everyone thought was a genius – should disappear without trace? Shouldn't at least something of you be left behind? The water would crumple it and erase all the writing, so that even if it was found, nobody would recognise what it was.

Especially not mum and dad, because you've had it hidden the whole time beneath your bed, convinced that was the only place in the house where they wouldn't find it.

No. You can't take the Book of Lists with you. You'll have to leave it on the bank. Let them find it. Let something remain. It's highly unlikely mum and dad will find it, but probably children from Kuželj, who often come to swim here, as it's easier to get in here than elsewhere.

And if they then take it to your parents, fine. Let them read your lists.

Maybe then they'll understand what they did to you.

You hide the Book of Lists beneath the nearest tree, covering it with yellowed leaves left over from the previous year; the first rain might uncover it and soak it. But deep inside, you suddenly feel that it's not important, that you're not even interested.

For nothing that happens after your death will be part of your life.

You'll feel nothing more.

Of that you're convinced.

You wade into the water. It's cold. In the middle of the summer, in the middle of the day, in a heat that permeates everything, the Kolpa is cold – so cold that you start to shiver when the water reaches your knees. But it was no different when you came here to swim, which you did often. It was perhaps even colder. It never bothered you then.

Why does it bother you now?

Because in your thoughts, your heart, your soul, your body, is something foreign, something unknown. A fear that it worse than all the fears you remember. And a stubbornness that is stronger than anything you were capable of in your life so far, before or after the Unfortunate Event.

You hurry, for it to be over as soon as possible.

Fully dressed, you wade to the middle of the river. To the deep part, where your feet no longer touch the bottom and you have to swim. But you don't swim.

You sink.

Before your head disappears beneath the surface, on the Croatian side of the river you see a young man, staring towards you. Are you mistaken, or is he really getting ready to enter the water?

A refugee. One of the many who swim across the river every day.

Alone. One of the few who doesn't have company.

You, too, are a refugee, you think. You are fleeing the war that is raging inside you, fleeing the horrors that are the total of the events in your life.

You go under, you open your mouth, you take a deep breath and let the water start to flow into your throat. And your lungs.

You are suffocating. It doesn't hurt, but the feeling is not a pleasant one.

You'd like to breathe, but you can't.

You pass out.

17.

Guardian angel

And find yourself in paradise.

Branches are dangling above your head and the sun's rays are pulsing through them, caressing you in waves. You seem to be wet through, but the heavenly sunshine is warming and drying you.

You are embraced by a feeling of blessedness.

Which doesn't last long.

For soon you start to choke again, you can't breathe, you are losing consciousness. You want to get out, out, out into the air and the light, back to life, you thrash your legs and arms and try to raise yourself, but you can't.

You are trapped by your shirt, which is caught on a sharp rock under the water and is preventing you from returning to life.

Then you feel someone's mouth on yours. You do not doubt that it is the kiss of your guardian angel.

But no.

It is not a kiss, but something is being sucked out of you. You are turned on your stomach and someone pounds your back. They turn you back over and again suck something from your lungs.

Water, which suddenly pours from you.

And then you see the face of your guardian angel above you.

From close up.

His eyes are brown. His hair is black and curly. He is young, maybe a few years older than you. Unshaven.

But certainly no younger than nineteen.

His nose is bent and there is a scar on his left cheek. His skin is slightly darker than yours. He is not black, far from it. Maybe just suntanned.

His eyes are full of amazement.

'Do you speak English?' he asks you.

It doesn't seem odd to you that angels in Heaven speak English. Hasn't English been for some time the universal language of communication on Earth?

So why not in Heaven, as well?

Except, of course, you think, if you're not in Heaven, but in Hell.

Whatever, you cannot lie, you should not.

So you reply: 'Yes.'

'Thank God for that,' the face of the angel (or devil?) stretches into a barely discernible smile. Whether for good or bad, you continue the conversation in English. You can't help noticing that you each have a different accent.

His seems a bit better than yours.

That's not unusual, for angels are sure to go to the best schools.

Devils, as well. Perhaps even to better ones.

And both to better ones than ordinary mortals.

Who cannot believe that they have ended up in Heaven, or perhaps Hell, when all their life they have believed that after death there is only a big Nothing.

'Are you my guardian angel?' you ask the unknown face above you.

'I'm not,' replies the stranger. 'Do you need him?'

'Very much,' you reply.

'Why did you go into the river, if you can't swim?'
'Of course I can swim. I went into the river to drown myself.'
'Bad idea,' replies the face. 'Death comes too soon even without help.'
'I have my reasons,' you say.
'You can have a thousand, but none is good enough.'
'What's your name?'
'Ahmed. I'm from Syria. And you?'
You're not in paradise. This is not a guardian angel in front of you. He is a refugee. He pulled you out of the water. You're grateful to him. The decision to drown yourself was not a good one.

You go over to the tree where you hid the Book of Lists beneath a pile of leaves, dig it out and go back to Ahmed, who is sitting soaked though in the sunlight.

'We've got to dry out,' he says, 'before we go on.'
'On to where?'
'Wherever,' he replies. 'It's important not to stay in one place. You need to keep moving forward. Standing still means death.'

You show him the Book of Lists and explain that you have written there everything that is important in your life. So that you don't forget. For since the Unfortunate Event, you forget things. You write things in lists, which represent a story for you. And when your head is overcome by emptiness, you leaf through the book, reading this and that, and after a while you get the feeling that you have a past, that you have a life.

You flip through the Book and read some lists to Ahmed. In the hope that from them he will form a picture of you.

You tell him that you once lived in Kočevje, but then mum and dad decided to move to an out-of-the-way village beside the River Kolpa.

Dad kept his job in Kočevje, while mum got a job as a secretary to the deputy mayor in Kostel. They had to buy another car. You go to the nearest school in Fara by bus. You prefer walking there across the hills and through the woods. On the way you see a lot of animals, including bears. You once even sat with a friendly bear beneath a tree and ate a banana together that you had in your bag.

You carefully read out to him a list of bad thoughts about mum and dad.

And a list of good thoughts about mum and dad.

And a list of good thoughts about Miss Pavla.

And a list of stupid things you have read or seen on the television.

And a list of the friends you had in Kočevje, before the Unfortunate Event.

And a list of cruel things the other kids at the school in Fara say about you, even though the teacher punishes them for it.

And a list of special abilities you developed after the Unfortunate Event.

Among them is the ability to learn foreign languages quickly. And to imitate accents. You can speak English with an American, Irish, Scottish, Australian and South African accent.

As a matter of fact, you wonder, is that the only special ability you developed after the Unfortunate Event?

An unusual ability, which in Laze is not much use to you.

And all your other abilities have been reduced by three-quarters or more.

You suddenly notice a police van coming along the road from Petrina.

You get scared that you will lose the friend who saved your life and who is, now that Piggy has gone, your only friend.

You have seen too often how the police catch refugees, bundle them in the van and take them who knows where.

'Hide in the bushes!' You push Ahmed towards the undergrowth beneath the riverside trees.

Ahmed, too, has spotted the police vehicle and doesn't hesitate

One, two, three and he's gone.

The vehicle stops and two police officers, one young, the other older, with a moustache, come along the grassy path towards you. They look at you for some time.

Then the older one with the moustache asks you what you are doing.

'I'm learning stuff for an exam,' you lie, showing them the Book of Lists you have in your hand.

'Where are you from?' asks the younger one.

'Laze,' you point in that direction. 'Up there, beneath the rock face.'

'Have you seen any refugees?'

'I often do,' you reply. 'But not today.'

'Why are you all wet?' the older one wants to know.

'I had a swim.'

'Dressed?' he asks in surprise.

'I always swim with my clothes on,' you claim. 'I'm not allowed in the sun. My mum says I could get skin cancer.'

'Your mum's a clever one, is she?' says the older officer, with a smirk. 'What does she do?'

'Secretary to the deputy mayor of Kostel,' you reply.

'Come on,' says the young officer, pulling the other one back towards the road.

They quickly return to the police vehicle and drive towards Kuželj.

Ahmed cautiously crawls out of the bushes and thanks you.

'I ought to thank you,' you reply. 'You saved my life. From now on, I am your servant.'

'I don't need a servant,' says Ahmed.

'Then your slave,' I say.

'That even less,' replies Ahmed.

From the Book of Lists, you read out what you wrote about the film *The Eagle,* which you saw on television.

At the time of the Roman Empire, at Hadrian's Wall in the north of England, a young centurion arrives who wants to find out why his father lost a statuette of the Golden Eagle, a symbol of the greatness of Rome, among the wild tribes north of the wall, bringing shame on his family. In the local arena there is a duel between a giant with a spear and a skinny prisoner who is half his size and is a member of the Brigante tribe that lives on the north side of the wall.

Of course, the giant soon has him on his back and raises his spear to pierce his heart. But he has to wait for the public to approve the death of the defeated one. Because he is a 'savage', the majority give a thumbs-down sign, meaning 'death'. Not the majority, actually, but all of them.

Except the centurion, who thinks that the killing of the unarmed youngster before the eyes of the crowd is unworthy of Roman honour. So he gives a thumbs-up, which means 'life'. Because he is a centurion, his decision has a decisive influence and the rest of the crowd also give a thumbs-up sign. The lad thanks the centurion and says that in return for his life, he must become his slave. Together, they go among the wild tribes to the north and return with the Golden Eagle, which restores the centurion's family's honour and his 'slave', who in reality has already become his friend, is officially granted his freedom and together they go forward to new adventures.

'A good film,' says Ahmed. 'But Roman times ended long ago. We can't look to old habits, we have to live in the present. Which in many ways are a lot worse than Roman times.'

'In spite of that, I want to become your slave,' you say.

'More than anything else, I need a friend.'

Above all, he adds, he hasn't eaten for some days.

Could you get him a piece of bread?

You quickly make three decisions.

That you will, regardless of what he said, secretly play the role of his slave. For he saved your life.

That at the same time you will be his best friend.

And that you will ensure his safety.

18.

The fate of pigs

Because evening is drawing near and the sun is setting behind the Gorski Kotar hills and your clothes are already dry, you can start to move. But it is still very light, you'd easily be spotted, and Ahmed recognised as a refugee, and the police called, and you would quickly lose the friend who you have promised to protect.

Systematically, as is your habit since the Unfortunate Event, you make a list of the possibilities.

And you decide that you and Ahmed will sleep in the hay in the barn at the old house, where your Piggy lived for some time. No one goes there.

And that you will go there when it gets dark and is safe.

That you will go home, tell you parents that you've been down to the Kolpa for a swim and that you slept for a while under a tree on the riverbank. In spite of that, you're still tired and will go to bed early.

When mum and dad start to watch their latest series on the television (a Turkish one, at mum's request; dad will fall asleep), you'll sneak into the kitchen, put whatever you can lay your hands on into a plastic carrier bag and take it secretly to the old barn, where Ahmed can eat his fill for the first time in ages.

When it gets dark, you lead Ahmed to the barn beside the old house, which is full of hay and suitable for sleeping, and ask him to wait. You leave the Book of Lists with him. Mum's not at home, she's gone somewhere in the car, maybe to a meeting with the deputy mayor. Dad's sitting dozing in an armchair in front of the television; whatever he was watching was evidently so boring that it sent him to sleep.

That's good! No need to explain anything to anyone!

You put at least half of what you find in the fridge into a plastic bag. Probably mum will miss some things, but you don't care. You take a loaf of white bread from the pantry.

In passing, you pick up a torch in the hall, because there's no electricity in the barn.

'I'm going to bed,' you shout through the living room door.

'Okay,' you hear dad's reply – you obviously woke him up.

However, you don't go to your room, but very quietly open the front door, closing it noiselessly behind you, and hurry towards the old house.

In the barn, you turn on the torch and in the beam of light you see Ahmed, sitting on the hay looking glum and worried. You put the torch on an old wooden crate and start taking the food out of the plastic bag, laying it at Ahmed's feet.

Bread, salami, cheese, pate, apples, bananas, tinned fish. The best you could do for now.

In the light of the torch, you see Ahmed's face spread into a smile.

Then he asks you if there is any pork in the pate. No, you shake your head, it's not proper salami, it's made from chicken.

'I'm a Muslim,' says Ahmed, 'and I don't eat pork.'
'I don't, either.'

You tell him that your parents murdered your best friend Piggy and forced you to eat his roast blood. So you will never, ever again touch pork. Never!

Even more, you will devote your life to liberating pigs from farms where they wait in insupportable conditions to be slaughtered. You'll go around the world and you won't stop until you have freed all the pigs on all the continents.

You don't know if you'll succeed, but you are determined to try.

You ask him why Muslims don't eat pork.

As he hungrily stuffs food inside him, he gives you reasons, which you write in the Book of Lists.

Pigs are dirty. They are fattened on rubbish dumps and fed on swill and other things that you wouldn't give to other animals.

Why don't Christians eat dogs? Is it then difficult to understand why Muslims and Jews don't eat pigs?

Is there a law telling people, regardless of their religion, that they must eat pigs?

Islam does not permit the raising and killing of pigs.

Modern, particularly educated Muslims do not necessarily follow all the old-fashioned prohibitions and some even drink alcohol, but no one touches the flesh of pigs.

He doesn't, either.

'Would you eat a cat?' he asks you. 'Would you eat a rat? Would you eat a snake? A spider? A toad?'

Of course not, you reply. And you understand why he doesn't want to eat pork. He has every right not to. Like you, whose best friend was a pig.

It seems that Ahmed can't believe your best friend was a pig.

You tell him the whole story again.

And add: 'From now on, my life's mission is to liberate all the pigs in the world.'

'How many are there?' he asks.

You open the Book of Lists.

The number of pigs being made to suffer in tiny cages until they are ready for slaughter, being butchered and sold in supermarkets, is beyond anything you could have imagined.

– 433 million in China.
– In the European Union 150 million.
– In the USA, 73 million.
– In Brazil, 36 million.
– In Russia, 22 million.
– In Canada, 14 million.
– In Mexico, 11 million.
– In Japan, 10 million.
– And so on.

Altogether, the countries of the world are raising 770 million pigs. Almost a billion! With the intention of slaughtering them and turning them into cutlets, sausages and other meat products, which people then eat, digest and excrete into the toilet.

You found a description for that.

'The processing of life into faeces.' You wrote an essay about it. You sent it to Miss Pavla and asked her to send it to the principal at the start of the school year. You entitled it *Pig Genocide*.

The principal didn't respond.

So, you're not going back to school.

You've decided to go around the world, liberating pigs.

Ahmed says nothing for a while. Then he shakes his head.

'You'll liberate 770 million pigs?'

You nod.

'Won't you think it over?'

You tell him that your mission has already started. You liberated seven pigs belonging to your grandfather, who lives in Kuželj, down in the valley. They went across the bridge to Croatia. Maybe they have already reached the coast and are swimming in the Adriatic. Nobody will slaughter them, roast them, fry them and eat them.

They'll be free.

Like most of the people in the world are free.

'Are they really?' says Ahmed in surprise. 'I didn't know that.'

19.

How 'great' were the great ones

Ahmed suddenly becomes sad.
Gloomy.
You think that he might be cheered up by one of the stories that you used to tell schoolmates during school holidays. You amused them by quoting from unusual lists. Even the biggest hooligans and brawlers liked to listen.

Most often, you told your stories when twenty of you slept together in the big room in the hostel. When, tired from swimming and the heat, one or another would almost always ask you to tell them some interesting facts. And always others added their voices to the request.

As a bedtime story, they said.

That's how it was last year, too, when your class went to a hostel near Poreč in Istria for five days.

What did you tell your schoolmates in the hostel dormitory late in the evening?

You think that Ahmed, who is not all that tall, might like best the story of how 'great' those who went down in history really were.

From the Book of Lists, you read him the following data:
– Queen Victoria, who reigned over an empire on which 'the sun never set', was 152 centimetres tall.
– Napoleon, who conquered half of Europe, was 167 centimetres tall.
– Yuri Gagarin, the first man in space, was 157 cm.
– Alexander Pope, the great English poet, was 137 cm.
– Pablo Picasso, the great artist, was 162 cm.
– Honoré de Balzac, the great French writer, was 157 cm.
– Stalin, Soviet dictator, was 168 cm.
– Voltaire, the French writer, was 160 cm.
– Tutankhamun, Egyptian Pharaoh, was 167 cm.
And how 'great' was Alexander the Great?
– 152 cm., less than most of the Greeks of his time.
And Churchill?
– 169 cm.
And Vladimir Putin?
– 169 cm.
And famous footballers?
– Maradona 165 cm, Lionel Messi 170 cm, Pele 172 cm.
And how tall (supposedly) was Jesus Christ?
– 132 cm.
'What about Mohamed?' Ahmed asks. 'Have data for him?'
You must admit that you haven't.
At the same time, it strikes you that maybe Ahmed would be interested how 'great' some people were, in terms of their character rather than their height.
You give him two examples from the Book of Lists:
– Martin Luther, the father of Protestantism, was anything but a friendly uncle who it would be nice to stay with for a week or two beside the sea. His intolerance to everything and everybody outside of his religious reforms was stunning, even at a time when intolerance was the rule, rather than

the exception. In 1525, when German peasants revolted and demanded their basic rights, he viciously attacked them in an essay entitled *Against the Murdering and Thieving Hordes of Yokels*. When his wife complained about their servants, he said: 'We need to deal with them in the Turkish way: so much work for so much food, like the Pharaoh did with the Israelis in Egypt. When the Jews failed to join his religious reforms in any numbers, he published an essay recommending that they be deported to Palestine; in any case, their synagogues should be burned to the ground and all their books seized.'

– Thomas Edison, who invented the lightbulb, was no less unpleasant.

He was convinced that ethics was one thing, business another, and that there was no connection between them. The duty of a businessman was to look after his interests and not give a damn about others, he said. His employees had to work long hours in chaotic and dangerous conditions, and he paid them just enough to stop them going elsewhere. He lived in his laboratory, as if he didn't have a family. Both his wives suffered from depression and his oldest son became an alcoholic, eventually committing suicide.

'No parents are perfect,' you add.

20.

From the Book of Lists

'And what else did you tell your schoolmates in the hostel?' Ahmed asks, evidently satisfied with what you've told him so far.

You're glad that you've managed to put him in a better mood. So, you give yourself a compliment by saying that there was never a night when you didn't entertain your curious schoolmates with unusual facts until one in the morning.

Some of them believed every word you said, others said that at least half of what you told them was made up.

Because you couldn't help noticing that some of your schoolmates were envious of your knowledge of everything, especially those who were less gifted, you tried one evening to console them with a list of famous and successful people who didn't exactly do well at school.

You also read that list to Ahmed.

– As a child, Albert Einstein, one of the greatest scientists of all time, was a disaster: until he was nine years old, he spoke so slowly, saying syllables rather than talking, that his parents thought he was retarded. Even later, he responded to questions after a long pause, as if he didn't know what he wanted to say. In secondary school, the principal advised him to leave, as it was more than clear that, with the exception of maths, he wasn't interested in anything and that he would achieve nothing in life, not even anything average. He twice failed the entrance exam for the polytechnic in Zűrich. And then after he graduated, he couldn't get a job without sooner or later losing it. And then – what a miracle!

– Pablo Picasso was an even bigger disaster in school than Einstein was, for nothing interested him apart from painting. When his father removed him from school at the age of ten, he could barely read and write. The tutor hired to get him into secondary school despaired after a few months, for Picasso kept on stubbornly insisting that he would not learn maths. He passed the exam for art school with excellent grades, but soon left the school because he was bored. Later, in Madrid and Paris, he sporadically studied painting privately, but he later said that no school had ever been of any use to him.

– Thomas Alva Edison made a terrible impression on everyone, except his indulgent mother. His first teacher described him as a scatterbrain and his father tried to convince him that he was simply an idiot. His school principal told his parents that he was below average and would achieve nothing in life. But his mother encouraged him to read and, in the end, he patented more than a thousand inventions.

How would we live without the lightbulb? Maybe someone else would have invented it.

But who?

More, more! demanded your schoolmates, who the school regarded as untalented.

You felt that your stories were consoling them, giving them hope, and so you told them more:

– the school failures of the composer Puccini (who even his first music teacher gave up on in despair),

– Henry Ford (when he finished school, he could barely read and write),

– Charles Darwin (who told his father that nothing interested him apart from shooting, dogs and rat hunting),

– Isaac Newton (who some see as the greatest mind of all time, but in school he had terrible grades, and showed himself to be incapable of running the family farm, which for him and for science was a blessing, otherwise he'd never have been sent to university),

– Émile Zola, the initiator of Realism literature, failed his exams in language and literature at the Sorbonne, although not in science and maths, which hurt him so much that he wrote to a friend that he was ‹the greatest ignoramus in the world›.

So that Ahmed appreciated how much your schoolmates valued your stories, you tell him that the most enthusiastic was Boxer, the worst pupil in the class, who in reality didn't like you and was always insulting and teasing you. In your stories, he sensed a possibility that he would stop being the duty 'idiot' and that he could go down in history as a 'genius', although nothing interested him and he behaved aggressively and negatively, not only towards smarter pupils, but also to the teachers.

'You're great,' he once said to you during the seaside holiday visit.

Not in front of the others, but in secret, in the toilet, where he had dragged you only to tell you this. You were convinced that even Boxer, your greatest enemy, would soon become your friend.

You were glad.
You didn't want enemies.
You wanted everyone you came into contact with in your life to be your friend.
Including, perhaps even most of all, Boxer.
'And?' Ahmed asks. 'Did he become your friend?'

21.
The Unfortunate Event

'Sadly not,' you reply. 'But it was Boxer who forever changed my life.'

You know that the moment has come when you must entrust Ahmed with the most important piece of information about you.

Besides being able to keep your schoolmates awake until one a.m., sometimes even to two a.m., by talking about your lists, you had the unfortunate habit of snoring loudly in your sleep. Thus depriving some, although not all, of sleep when they most needed it.

You didn't do this deliberately. That's how it was. The doctor that mum took you to said there was something wrong with your sinuses, throat and vocal cords – with all the organs that facilitate breathing. And there was no indication that the situation would improve. The only thing you could hope for, said the doctor, is to find a wife who wasn't bothered by your loud, at times very noisy, snoring.

But it did annoy quite a few of your schoolmates in the seaside hostel.

Most of all Boxer, who at least twice a night warned you to stop snoring, or he'd beat you up, or ensure in some other way that you would stop depriving him of sleep.

And at least twice a night, and again during the day, you apologised and explained to him that, unfortunately, it wasn't in your power to do anything about it, for when you were asleep you didn't even know you were snoring.

Nature had given you a problem and you would have to live with it to the end of your days.

And you weren't the only one who snored. There were a lot more snorers than people might imagine. Snoring is one of those nuisances that denies us the right to see ourselves as anything special, better, worth more than animals.

'You,' Boxer shouted one night, 'you're an animal! You're a pig! Someone needs to stop you committing this violence against us!'

He grabbed you by the shoulders and lifted you into a sitting position. Then he grabbed hold of your ears and banged your head against the wall behind the bed so hard and for so long that you passed out.

When you finally came round, you realised that there was something wrong in your head.

The banging against the wall had concussed your brain and shaken it up so badly that you no longer had access to certain parts of it.

That was the Unfortunate Event that made you into what you are now.

After every possible test, the specialists said that it wasn't completely clear to them what had happened. They comforted you by saying that time could heal many things. Most cases of brain damage are temporary. Maybe just to reassure your mum and dad, they said there would be fluctuations. Sometimes your condition would be almost normal, your brain would work almost as well as it did before the Unfortunate Event, but other times, probably more often, you would find it difficult to keep up at school.

And that would need to be accepted.

It was impossible to predict how things would develop. The best thing was to keep hoping, but at the same time to be prepared for the worst. There was a possibility, although a very small one, that the condition would worsen.

Sadly, medicine cannot perform miracles.

At least, not in your case.

22.
Bombs and history

'I thought something like that must have happened,' says Ahmed.

'I'm sorry I didn't tell you before,' you reply. 'Didn't I seem a bit strange to you?'

'We're all strange,' he says, to comfort you. 'Each in our own way.'

You're both tired, it's time to rest. When you've settled down in the hay, Ahmed says that he also has some lists.

Or in fact, just one. All the others are consequences of that one.

You ask him to tell you.

And he tells you how, where and how thirty of his relatives died.

It's hard for you to imagine that he had so many!

At the same time, maybe you have more than you have met in your life. Uncles, aunts and cousins on both mum's and dad's side, plus others. Maybe you'd find at least fifteen if you made the effort.

But in Slovenia, family ties are not as strong as in Syria. You like that.

It would be hard for you to find the energy and willpower to deal with a horde of relatives that you've never met before. The New Year cards that mum and dad send to some of them are more than enough.

In Syria, things are different. A war has been raging there for years.

But for thirty of his relatives to die?

It seems impossible.

You write his list in the Book, so that you don't forget.

Every written record is a document. And documents are evidence of what happens in the world.

You write that Ahmed had a father and mother, two grandfathers, two grandmothers, four sisters, three brothers, five uncles and aunts, and twelve cousins.

Total: thirty.

After thinking it over, it doesn't seem so many.

Of the thirty, the only one still alive is his twenty-year-old brother. He managed to get away and travelled to London.

What happened to the others?

After a long silence, Ahmed tells you.

The grandfather and grandmother on the mother's side lived in the village of Hatla, near Deir el-Zour.

On 11 June 2013, two grandchildren were visiting them – Ahmed's sisters.

They came to help their grandma because their granddad was ill.

On that day, Sunni rebels attacked the village and killed thirty people, supposedly because the day before Shiite pro-government fighters, who were camping in Hatla, had allegedly attacked them.

During the attack, the rebels killed many villagers. Old people, men, women and children.

They set fire to more than twenty houses.

Of thirty relatives, Ahmed was left with twenty-six.

But not for long.

On the last day of August in the same year, the number was reduced to fifteen.

In the rebel suburb of Ghouta, near Damascus, there lived two uncles and their wives, six daughters and three sons.

The youngest daughters, Ahmed's cousins, were three and four years old, the boys twelve, eight and five. One of the uncles was a doctor, the other an engineer.

On the last day of August, missiles were fired at the eastern part of the city, which released the poisonous gas Sarin.

The warring sides could not agree how many people had been killed. One side said 280, the other more than 1700.

For Ahmed, only one number mattered: eleven relatives killed by poison gas.

He hoped that he would at least be left with fifteen.

Vain hope.

On 11 December 2013, two rebel groups, the Islamic Front and Al-Nusra, attacked the industrial area of Adra, a small town north-east of Damascus.

They attacked the buildings where the workers and their families lived. The rebels massacred – each group separately – Alawites, Druze, Christians and Shiites.

Some were shot, others beheaded. They killed whole families, including babies.

As well as 40 civilians, 18 members of a pro-government militia died.

In factories in Adra, in various posts, nine of Ahmed's relatives were employed. Two uncles, five cousins and two cousins.

The number of surviving relatives fell to six: father, mother, older brother, two sisters and the grandfather on father's side. The grandmother, meanwhile, died of natural causes.

The older brother decided that he would join the flood of refugees heading for Europe. His mother and father protested, but one day he simply disappeared.

Ahmed thought about following him. Then, he decided that he would first complete English secondary school, which he attended in Aleppo. If he finished school, it would be easier to get a job in Europe, when he followed his brother.

His father, mother, grandfather and two sisters lived in Raqqa, in the north of Syria. His father was a maths teacher and his mother taught history in the same school. His sisters were pupils at the school.

This was also the school that Ahmed attended before his parents sent him to the English secondary school in Aleppo.

Two rebel groups took over Raqqa, driving out the government forces. Disputes arose, which ISIS (Islamic State), led by Abu Bakr al-Baghdadi, took advantage of to infiltrate institutions and to take control. Abu Bakr proclaimed Raqqa as the capital of the Islamic State, which aimed eventually to take over the whole Islamic world and to launch a 'holy war' against all non-believers.

The father lost his job. He was forced to collect taxes from all those who did anything in the town.

The sisters had to marry ISIS fighters, even though they were only twelve and thirteen years old. The mother remained at home, but one day when her husband was not at home ISIS fighters came to the house intent on raping her. The grandfather begged them to spare her. He fell on his knees before them. They smashed his skull with a rifle butt. Both of them died.

All this, Ahmed found out from a neighbour, who managed to get away. He did not want to return to Raqqa, for they would have killed him, as well. He stayed in Aleppo because he wanted to finish school.

War was raging all around, people were suffering, dying. And almost no one understood why, or even less, who was on which side.

Russian planes were bombing the positions of rebels, who were backed by the Americans and their allies.

The world stood on the threshold of a third world war.

But then the Russians and Americans joined together to fight the Islamic State, which was cutting off prisoners' heads in front of video cameras and posting the images online. The world had never seen such horrors. When Ahmed finished the English school and got a certificate, he decided to go to Raqqa to try and rescue the relatives he had left.

Two younger sisters and his father.

It was too late.

In June 2017, American, British and French planes began intensive bombing of Raqqa, which al-Baghdadi had proclaimed as the capital of his Caliphate. From June to October, over five months, the Americans alone dropped 30,000 bombs on the town.

The destruction was total. The Islamic State was defeated, many of its fighters killed, but also many civilians who had no connection with anything.

In a single bomb attack, the Badran family lost 39 of its members, the Hashish family 18 members, the Fayad family 16.

He never received any information about the fate of his sisters and father.

He knew only that they were killed by bombs.

Amnesty International condemned the American, British and French bombing of Raqqa as a war crime. The attackers should have taken measures to protect the civilian population.

They did not do this, they wanted to destroy the whole town.

Soon after, he got a text message from his brother in London.

'Come as soon as possible. I am seriously ill. I'd like to see you before I die.'

23.

Sometimes you have to cry

That was the list that your rescuer, Ahmed, offered you. And that is roughly how you write it down in your Book of Lists. Then you read it through again and check that you haven't made any mistakes in turning it into Slovene.

For in the Book of Lists, mistakes are not allowed.

'Now you tell me some list,' says Ahmed. 'Didn't you say that lists are stories?'

That's true. But instead of reading something interesting, encouraging or entertaining from your Book of Lists, something shifts inside you.

You burst into tears.

You don't remember the last time you cried. Since the Unfortunate Event, not once. You couldn't. Not even when Piggy was murdered. Something froze inside you, surrounding your heart and soul like a stone wall. But now, when Ahmed told of the relatives who had been killed, the wall came tumbling down. As if one of the American or British bombs that killed the last of Ahmed's relatives had fallen on it.

You're surprised. And scared.

'What's wrong?' Ahmed asks.

Nothing, you think. Nothing is wrong.

Quite the opposite.

It seems that, along with the tears, melted cement is also flowing from you. And all the weight that after the Unfortunate Event, if not also before, you carried inside you. Carted around the world without hope that things would ever be different.

And now ...

Now you feel that something has changed inside. As if you have looked through the window and seen a different, more real world.

Suddenly, without really being aware of what you are doing, you put your arms around Ahmed and hug him.

He saved your life.

He didn't have to. He could easily have let you drown. You're not one of his relatives. He could have crossed the river and continued on his way.

Asked for asylum. Gone on to Austria, Germany, Sweden.

But he stopped and pulled you from the water.

It's thanks to him you are still alive!

The decision to drown yourself was the most stupid you ever took.

'Why are you crying?' Ahmed asks and slowly begins to loosen himself from your hug, which is smothering him.

'Because ...'

You cannot, you do not know how to continue.

How trivial were your lists in comparison with his!

How stupid, petty, sulky you are because you lost your friend Piggy. Ahmed lost thirty relatives, who are not pigs, but people. Aren't people worth more than pigs? Or at least as much?

Especially relatives? Brothers, sisters? Granddads, grandmas?

Aren't your mum and dad worth more than your Piggy?

'How can I help you?' you ask Ahmed.

'Help me get to London,' he says.

Almost in passing, as if he is talking about the weather, without any undertone to indicate that he wants something in return for saving you from the river.

'I'd be happy to,' you reply, with no idea of how you might be able to help him. 'I'll be your friend. The best you ever had.'

'Don't become friends with an elephant herder, unless you have room for his elephant,' replies Ahmed with a smile. Without explaining what his words mean.

'I owe you that,' you say. 'If you hadn't come here from Syria at the right moment, the river would already be carrying me towards the Black Sea.'

'It wouldn't,' says Ahmed with a shake of the head. 'You'd have got stuck on the rocks. You would be in paradise. In a special part where they look after the mentally handicapped.'

'How do you know I'm mentally handicapped?'

'You told me.'

'What about you?' you ask him. 'How did you get from Syria to here. It's a long way.'

'It's not exactly close.'

'I can't imagine how you did it.'

24.

On the way to his brother

Ahmed replies that he almost didn't.

And he goes through the list of events he experienced on the way from Syria to the part of the Kolpa where you tried to drown yourself

You write it down.

From Syria he headed for Turkey with a large group of refugees. They got to the shore of the Aegean Sea. There, like all the rest, he had to pay one thousand dollars to the owner of a boat that transported people to the Greek island of Lesbos.

Luckily, he wasn't without money; while studying, he had sometimes worked part time and his father had sometimes sent him money before he was killed by British and American bombs. He was afraid of the sea, but he had no choice.

There were too many people crammed onto the boat and it almost tipped over during its night voyage.

Fortunately, it didn't, although three children and four old men fell into the sea and drowned.

There was no one to pull them out of the water. The skipper of the boat refused to stop.

On Lesbos, Ahmed slept for some nights on the streets of the main town, Mytilene, along with other refugees – not just Syrians, but also Iraqis, Iranians, Afghans. He had a smart phone with him so that he could keep his brother informed about where he was and how he was progressing.

After a few days, he was able to get onto one of the ferries taking refugees from the islands of Lesbos, Kos, Kalymnos and Leros to Piraeus on the Greek mainland. From there, he hitchhiked to the centre of Athens, where more than a thousand refugees were living in the parks and on the streets.

No one wanted to go to England as he did, they were all heading for Germany, Denmark or Sweden; they had heard that it was best there and that they were welcome.

'*Willkomen*,' the German Chancellor had evidently said.

But they first had to get to the Schengen border with Hungary or Slovenia. Inside the Schengen area, they had been told, there were no borders and you could go where you wanted. In the country where you wanted to stay, you asked for asylum.

But the news soon came that Hungary had closed its border and then that Macedonia was guarding its border. He was stuck in Greece.

In Athens, he got to know an Afghan of about the same age, who convinced him that the safest route was through the Muslim parts of Europe. Through Albania, Kosovo, Bosnia and Herzegovina.

They travelled on together. And ended up in the Bosnian refugee camp at Velika Kladuša. There, too, most of the locals were Muslims: they were willing to help them, they got some clothes and food, which was hard to come by on the journey. And some advice about the way forward.

His friend from Afghanistan decided to ask for asylum in Bosnia and Herzegovina, as he wanted to stay among Muslims.

Ahmed would also have done that if his brother was not waiting for him in London.

And so, partly on foot, partly by bus, he had headed for the Croatian border. He crossed it in the middle of the night in the hope that he would avoid the police and be able to secretly continue his journey towards the Schengen border with Slovenia.

There, his troubles would be over.

That, at least, was what he concluded after listening to others.

It was different.

After crossing the Croatian border, he was stopped by police, who looked at his passport and set him back to Velika Kladuša. Once again, with the help of a mobile phone, which he had bought quite cheaply, after losing his own, from one of his older compatriots, he made a plan for a safer route across the Croatian border.

And once again, the same thing happened.

He knew that he could not give up. The third time, he succeeded. In the middle of a rainy night, he reached the River Kolpa, which separates Slovenia and Croatia. This was the area known as Bela Krajina, where the river is very wide. And deep. On the Slovene side there was a wire fence running along the river.

Although he couldn't swim and he wasn't sure whether he'd be able to get across the fence, he went into the river and began to wave his arms and legs around, as he had seen swimmers on the television do. He thought he would drown at any moment and so he was greatly surprised when he stayed on the surface.

In fear for his life, he had learned, within moments, to swim.

He found a hole cut in the fence on the Slovene side and crawled through it into the Schengen area of the European Union. There, because of what he had heard, he expected to be able to move freely as far as the west coast of France, where one way or another he would be able to smuggle himself into Britain.

Two minutes later, a police van drove past.

Ahmed asked for asylum. The police officers pretended not to understand and drove him across a nearby bridge back to Croatia. But he didn't remain there. The Croatian police sent him back to Bosnia, to Velika Kladuša.

He set off once again, this time rather differently. But again, he got to the Kolpa, which he would have to swim across, and again there was a fence on the other side. For the first time, he felt that Europe did not want him, and he began to worry that he would never reach his brother before he died.

This time, he didn't manage to swim across. As soon as he waded in, Croatian police pounced on him, pulled him to the bank, beat him on his back with truncheons, took away his mobile phone, which one of them stood on in his heavy boots, smashing it to pieces; they seized his passport, pulled his hair and slapped him, and sent him back to Velika Kladuša.

He knew that he must not stop. One way or another, he must reach his brother in London before he lost him, too.

In Velika Kladuša, one of the many Iraqi refugees advised him not to go to the same place, but to go farther west, until he reached the hill settlement of Delnice; from there, he could drop down into the Kolpa Valley, although not to the border crossing at Brod na Kolpi, but through the woods farther west. There, he could swim across the river, where it was shallow, and he would have the best chance of dodging the Slovene border police.

And once in Slovenia, he would be in the European Union, inside which there were no longer any borders or checks. Then, his only problem would be how to get from the Continent to Britain.

And to London. To his brother

Who no one would miss when he died.

Because he had no one else.

Except his younger brother.

25.

Preparing to cross Europe

Look through the window.
It's morning, the sun is shining, mum and dad have gone to work. Although you were with Ahmed in the barn at the old house, they didn't miss you; they were convinced you were in your room, sleeping.
And that you would make your own breakfast.
You can quietly return to the house and start getting ready for the journey.
To save the refugee Ahmed, who wants to reach his brother.
If the task is as exciting as the saving of Private Ryan, then you are embarking on something that will occupy a lot of pages in the Book of Lists.
You'll have to buy a new notebook.
You'll miss the orchard that is spread out before you. There are so many trees in it that you know intimately. And the view of the wooded slope behind the orchard and the steep hills of Gorski Kotar in the background, can you live without that?

It will be hard.

But you have no choice.

You go back to the old house, open the barn door and see that Ahmed is once more asleep.

You think that after all he has gone through, he must be terribly tired. Will he resent it if you wake him?

No, for twice during the night he said that you must set off early.

London is far.

And you have no idea how you'll get there.

You are glad when you see that he has opened his eyes and that you don't need to wake him.

'Are we going?' is all he says.

'Soon,' you reply.

He follows you to the house, you invite him into the kitchen and ask him if he'd like fried eggs for breakfast. You make him coffee, fry him three eggs, cut several slices of rye bread, join him at the table, watch how he stuffs the food into his mouth. He seems to be hungry. Even though he ate everything you brought him the evening before. He has been on the road a long time. There have been few times and places when he got something to eat. You're happy when you see how eager he is for the food you have prepared.

When he has finished, you ask him if he wants three more eggs.

He shakes his head. 'We must get going.'

He seems calm

You're not.

The biggest adventure of your life is in front of you.

Will you be up to it?

You're not sure. Ahmed doesn't have a passport, they took it from him, they took everything that he could use to prove who he is. They smashed his phone. He can't get in touch with anyone he knows. You have a passport, but you are under age and you can't officially cross the border without your parents' written permission, stamped by a notary. This isn't the case for countries inside Schengen, but you've heard on the television that even here they are carrying out border checks.

But what use to you is a passport, if Ahmed doesn't have one?

You'll have to get to London a different way.

Along secret routes.

So that no one stops you, no one catches you, no one locks you up.

Ahmed doesn't intend to ask for asylum in Austria, or Germany, or France.

He wants to get to London, regardless.

It's clear that you will have to work out the best route together. You will have to avoid all the pitfalls and dangers together.

And the route must lead past the biggest pig farm in Western Europe. You have agreed that on the way you will liberate as many imprisoned pigs as possible.

That was your condition and Ahmed accepted it.

'We'll need some money' he says.

'Why?' you ask in surprise. 'Will we sleep in hotels?'

'Maybe,' says Ahmed. 'How do I know. But we've got to eat. Otherwise we'll die before we even reach France.'

Of course, you think. How stupid that you didn't think of that.

How little you know. You have no idea of the dangers lurking on the way.

Ahmed will have to take most of the decisions. He has experience, whereas you have none. Except walking over the hills and through the woods to school.

109

And some encounters with bears.

You'll have to trust him.

So why is he saying that you have to help him? How could a 'dummy' like you help a refugee who is four years older, who completed English school and came from Syria to Europe?

Why does he even want you to go with him?

It's not clear.

Maybe he needs company. Maybe he thinks that you know Europe better than him. Because you are European. Maybe he feels obliged to take you with him because he wants to help a liberator of pigs.

But it might be altogether simpler than that: he needs money.

And he thinks that you can get it for him

You're not completely penniless, you've got some savings in an envelope you keep under your bed. You're earned it giving maths tuition before the Unfortunate Event and since then you haven't touched it. You also added some pocket money to it.

But 130 euros won't get you to the London.

Maybe mum and dad also have some money hidden in the house. Why would they carry it with them when they use their credit cards in shops?

You start looking. You go through all the drawers in their bedroom. Then the cupboards. You look underneath the mattress and beneath the bed. You check the pockets of clothes hanging in the wardrobe.

Then you search the living room, the pantry, the kitchen, the cellar, the attic. You open every box you find.

Nothing anywhere.

Mum and dad keep no money at home.

Then you think of the garage.

You ask Ahmed to stay in the kitchen and eat whatever he can find in the fridge, as it will be quite some time before you eat again.

You go to the garage. Sometimes dad's car is in there, but more often mum's. The other is parked beneath the nearest tree beside the road.

Now they are at work, the garage is empty.

Where did you get the idea that one of your parents is hiding money in the garage?

You've no clue. It's a feeling that has hooked you like a fish.

In the garage are two chests-of-drawers containing all sorts of things: tools, screws, engine oil, bottles of liquid for spraying on frozen windscreens. If you wrote all the items in the Book of Lists, you'd fill two pages, but the list would have no story.

But ...

When you pull out the lower drawer, the list becomes a story.

You don't pull it out to see what is in it, but you take it out to see what is underneath it. And beneath the bottom drawer is a brown envelope containing a heap of banknotes. More a wad than a heap, but the amount that you come to when you have twice counted the notes is not so small.

2500 euros!

Who is hiding money in this secret place?

Dad? Mum?

Why?

Whoever it is, they could have kept the money in the bank.

But you've no time for reflection. It seems right to you to seize the money.

26.

Funeral ceremony

Before you set off, you ask Ahmed to wait a little. You type into Google *Pig farms in Western Europe*. You need a list of the prisons from which you and Ahmed will rescue the four-legged prisoners.

For the first time ever, Google disappoints you. You find all sorts of information about pig farming in Germany, France, Britain and other countries, but whatever you type in, you cannot get a list of pig farmers with names and addresses.

Where will you find the pig farms?

You keep searching and searching. Ahmed asks if you will soon be finished, he's in a hurry to leave, but you still can't find anything. There's probably no reason why such a list should appear online. Pig farms are not tourist sights.

You tell Ahmed of your problem.

He doesn't know how to help.

Then he suggests that on the way, here and there, you can ask if there is a pig farm nearby. There are sure to be people who know, especially butchers and shopkeepers, for pig farms are not military secrets.

There's no reason for panic, there will be more than enough opportunities to liberate some pigs.

You're grateful to him.

You stuff into your rucksack two shirts, some trousers, three pairs of socks, three pairs of underpants, soap, a towel, a toothbrush and toothpaste, three pens and, of course, the Book of Lists.

Then you take a slightly larger rucksack from the pantry. Before the Unfortunate Event you used it when you went to the seaside. You put into it all the tins you find on the kitchen shelves, with baked beans, stew, sardines and tuna, as well as some apples and pears, and finally an untouched loaf of buckwheat bread.

Then you invite Ahmed into your parents' bedroom and open the door to the wardrobe where dad keeps his clothes. Ahmed is bigger than you, whereas your dad is medium size. You ask Ahmed to check whether any of dad's clothes fit him. It turns out that the trousers, shirts, t-shirts and jackets do – in fact, everything does. So, you stuff some spare clothes for him into the large rucksack.

'Are we going?' asks Ahmed.

Already impatient, you think.

You ask him for another half hour. You have decided to write your parents a goodbye letter. You're sure it's the right thing to do, as you will never see them again.

But when you sit down at the table and pick up a pen, another idea comes into your head.

You go down to the cellar and look for a spade. At the edge of the orchard, beneath the tree where mum and dad usually sit in their wicker chairs, reading the newspaper and magazines, you dig a hole. Not deep and not too wide. You

113

put down the spade and go into the cellar where there is a large freezer.

You take from it all the parts of your friend Piggy wrapped in plastic bags, even the liver and kidneys, but not the head, which granddad took, or the leg which mum and dad also gave to granddad so that he could cure it. One piece at a time, you put it in a bucket and go back to the hole you have dug, and you place all the pieces of your murdered friend in it.

Then you fill in the hole.

Ahmed sits on the grass watching you.

Then you go to the shed where dad keeps his tools. You find a long piece of wood, which you saw in two, and then you take a hammer and nails and make a cross. You sharpen the lower part with a knife, take the cross to the grave on the edge of the orchard and use the hammer to bang it into the earth, facing the house.

'Just a little longer,' you say to Ahmed.

You go into the house, find a cardboard box and cut off the sides you don't need so that you are left with a rectangular piece of cardboard. Then you go into your room, look through the photos you keep in a drawer, find the nicest one, at least you like it the most, and write on the piece of cardboard: *Here lies Piggy, my best friend.*

You return to the grave. You fix the inscription and the photo to the cross with drawing pins.

Ahmed gets up, comes closer and looks at the photograph.

On it, Piggy is sitting on his bottom, almost the way that dogs and cats sit, while you sit beside him with your arm around his neck.

Ahmed gives a bitter smile and says: 'I'll never understand Christians.'

And after a while: 'And probably, you'll never understand Muslims.'

'I'll try,' you reply.

27.
Through the woods to the road

You put the rucksacks on your backs, Ahmed the bigger, heavier one, lock the door and put the key under the stone among the flower pots, as you usually do. You touch the front door with your damp hand, knowing it's for the last time. And that you will never see the house, which was never a real home to you, again.
 Then you go along the road towards the old house.
 Something stops you. Ahmed, too.
 Have you got a plan for how to get to London?
 You haven't.
 You must avoid contact with the police.
 Ahmed must certainly avoid the police, because they would immediately put him into a refugee centre.
 Or return him once more to Croatia. Or to Bosnia.
 'Do you have a plan?' you ask Ahmed.
 'Get me to Austria,' he says, 'from there, I'll decide.'
 'On condition that we free some pigs on the way.'
 'Where?' Ahmed unexpectedly gets upset, for the first time since he pulled you from the Kolpa. 'Here?'

You know you must be doing something wrong. Ahmed's impatience with you hurts.

You offer him your phone. It is old and you don't remember the last time you used it, but the battery isn't empty, it's usable.

'Call your brother in London. Tell him we're coming.'

Now Ahmed gets even more upset.

'How can I call him when I don't know his number by heart? It was in the phone that the Croats smashed!'

You put the phone away. Ahmed has every right to get upset. You're not the only one to have suffered an injustice. Ahmed has suffered a much greater one. Maybe there are more monsters in this world than the ones you were afraid would crawl through your window while you were asleep.

Can you help the refugee who saved your life to reach his brother in London, without him ending up in jail?

You are increasingly doubtful that you'll succeed.

And who will be at fault for everything that goes wrong? You.

'Just a minute,' you say.

You sit on the roadside grass, your rucksacks on your backs.

You know that the greatest danger for Ahmed lies on the road from Osilnica to the border crossing at Petrina, along the fence which the government placed along the river, although not in every section, to stop refugees getting into Slovenia. There are police patrols constantly driving up and down that road.

Ahmed doesn't look like a local. He has curly hair and his beard is growing, because he couldn't shave on his journey. Who would see him as a Slovene or a European? If you went to Petrina along the road, you'd almost certainly get stopped by the police.

'What are we waiting for?' he asks.

'We'll go in the other direction,' you say. 'Through the woods and over the hill.'

You head back towards the house and then past the house towards Lojze's, who is usually in Ljubljana in the summer, and then along the narrow path to Lado's wooden weekend house, which is usually empty, and on towards the wood, which covers the slope to the top of the hill, and down the other side to the next hill, and onwards. It's hot, more than it usually is in the summer. Slovenia is in the grip of a heatwave.

It takes you two hours to reach your goal.

Tired and sweaty.

You rest for half an hour in the shade of the trees at the edge of the wood.

You watch the border crossing, which goes across the Kolpa to the village of Brod na Kolpi on the Croatian side. Tourists are returning from the Croatian coast, while others are waiting in line for the Croatian border police to let them through to the road that leads to the sea.

'I see you are writing everything in the Book of Lists,' says Ahmed. 'I understand why, and I wouldn't want to deprive you of your memories, without which none of us has a life, either good or bad.'

You agree.

'But since, somewhere on the way to London, we might fall into the hands of the guardians of European civilisation, who will very carefully examine your Book of Lists, please don't write anything specific in it. Neither our destination, nor what has happened so far, and please don't mention my brother in London or write down the names and locations of the pig farms from where we will, if things work out, release the pigs, because they could lock you up for that. Write things down in such a way that no one apart from you will understand.'

You're not convinced you'll be able to do that.

You will try, of course, although you're not sure what you're allowed to write and what not. But to write nothing is not possible. Your life since the Unfortunate Event is only accessible to you when you read the Book of Lists.

'I will,' you promise.

28.

The pig salesman

The journey to London begins without difficulty, your worries were unfounded. A hundred metres up from the border crossing at Petrina, above the petrol station, where tourists returning from holidays on the Dalmatian islands stop, you wait for the car that seems safest to Ahmed. With German registration. With only a driver. Who is bored and would welcome talking to a couple of hitchhikers.

He is happy when he invites you into his big black Mercedes; you on the front seat, Ahmed at the back. He is a friendly, middle-aged man with a moustache, who speaks English with a German accent and because your accent is almost perfectly English, he assumes you are both from England.

'Have you been at the seaside?' he asks, looking at Ahmed in the rear-view mirror. It seems he does not know how to connect Ahmed with you. 'School holidays? Going home?'

'Back to London,' you say. 'The Adriatic was lovely.'

'To London?' he sounds surprised. 'I thought you were English. I'm not going so far. And not in that direction.'

'Where are you going?' Ahmed asks.

'Berlin,' replies the man with the moustache. It doesn't escape you that he is slightly confused when he hears that Ahmed's accent is different from yours. 'I have to go slightly off my route and stop for a few hours in Frankfurt. You can go with me as far as there, if you want, and then carry on to Ostend or Calais. Ten hours' drive. At least I won't be bored.'

'That would be great,' says Ahmed.

'Actually,' you correct him, 'there are places we'd like to stop on the way. To see the sights. As far as Ljubljana will be enough.'

'Why?' asks Ahmed behind you. 'Frankfurt is ideal, almost half way to London. We can see the sights some other time. It would be crazy to turn down this opportunity.'

'You decide,' says the driver with a shrug, overtaking three cars.

Ahmed's arbitrary decision annoys you. You try to suppress your anger, as he did save your life and you promised to be his slave, but you agreed to free some pigs in the way to London.

Has Ahmed decided to ignore your agreement?

You wrack your brain for a solution. And as you do so, you are suffering terribly. Evidently Ahmed's only goal is to get to London as soon as possible, whereas yours is to free as many pigs as possible. You'd like to remind him of your agreement, but in the presence of this man who has generously offered you a lift, you cannot.

'To Ljubljana will be fine,' you repeat.

The moustached man looked once again at Ahmed in the rear-view mirror and asks: 'Your brother?'

'It would be hard for us to be brothers,' you reply. 'We're not even alike.'

'I noticed that,' says the man. 'Friends?'

'Guardian,' you reply, without really thinking it through. 'At the age of fifteen I can't travel across Europe on my own. He's an adult and is responsible for me.'

'Okay,' says the driver, 'but how can he be your guardian?' Ahmed, whose common sense had evidently returned, suddenly spoke up. 'We have the same dad and different mothers. Our dad was a British officer during the Allied attacks on Afghanistan. My mum died during British bombing of a suspected Taliban base. In reality, it was a market place in Kabul. My dad took me with him when he returned to England, where he married an Englishwoman and they had my younger brother. That's why now, when we're on holiday, I have their permission to be his guardian.'

'Interesting story,' said the moustached driver. 'There are probably quite a few like that.'

You look at him sideways and he shows no signs of disbelieving the tale.

You're grateful to Ahmed for solving a problem that seemed insoluble.

Then, conveniently, your driver asks which sights you'd like to see on the way back to London. If there weren't too many, he'd happily stop for an hour or two where they wanted, he wasn't in such a hurry.

'Pig farms,' you reply honestly, without thinking. 'In Slovenia, Austria, Germany, France, all the way to London.'

'Pig farms?!' the driver raises his voice, not in anger, but in surprise. 'Since when were pig farms tourist sights?'

'They are for us,' you reply, as if you've had a flash of inspiration. 'For others, they are maybe just a bad smell.'

'Wait, wait, wait,' says the man, sounding excited. 'You're interested in pig farms?'

'My brother isn't,' you reply. 'He's studying electronics. But I am. I'd like to become a dealer in pork products. I'm intending to go to agricultural college. And then maybe to do veterinary studies. I'm too young to know exactly what I want.'

The moustached German takes a deep breath and for a while says nothing.

'Shall I tell you what my profession is?' he says, turning to you.

'Please,' you reply.

'I'm a salesman. I sell German pork products to butchers and supermarkets across Europe. I'm just returning from a business trip to Croatia, where I managed to sell twice as many pigs as I expected. Do you want to do what I do? Putting aside that it's an almost incredible coincidence, I advise you to choose another career.'

You're amazed.

And you barely believe him. He must be joking.

Behind you, Ahmed lets out what sounds like mocking laughter.

'Why?' you want to know.

'Because pigs smell,' the man livens up. 'It's worst for those who feed them and clean them out. And also, the butchers who slaughter them. The stench makes its way even into the skin and clothes of those who sell them, even though they have no direct contact. I represent the biggest pig farm in Germany, Straathof's, south-west of Berlin, which is also the biggest in the EU. We have branches in other European countries. We raise a million and a half suckling pigs each year. Can you imagine? Although you're both young and maybe don't know what it means, I lost my wife because of pigs. In the middle of the night, in bed, she told me I smelled of pigs. I had visited farms a number of times to see what I'm selling across Europe, but I had never touched them. In spite of that, in bed, she detected a smell of pigs. And she said she couldn't stand it anymore. She became a vegan. She said she couldn't understand why so many living creatures had to be raised and then slaughtered. That it was a crime. And that we should just be eating walnuts, mushrooms, strawberries and things like that. And she left. So, don't mention pigs to me. I hate them. Stop talking about pigs.'

'Why do you sell them, then?' you ask.

'You're too young to understand. I'm sure your parents support you. What about me? In two years, I'll be sixty. Can I get a job as an architect? An engineer? A history teacher? Or even a vet? No. All doors are closed to me. Until I retire, I must persevere in the profession that disgusts me so much I often throw up. And you'd like to sell pork products?'

'I don't think pigs smell,' you say, feeling obliged to defend your Piggy. 'In fact, a pig was one of my best friends, until my parents slaughtered it for my birthday.'

'That's something different,' says the man. 'You can become friends with a cat, dog, a horse, a parrot, so why not with a pig? But I'm talking about the pig industry. It's a filthy business. Shall I tell you why you've chosen the wrong profession?'

'Please,' you say.

'I don't want to say anything bad about the country where I was born and live. And it's not the only one to raise pigs. But they raise the most in Europe. Last year, they sent 28 million pigs to foreign markets. At the same time, 60 million pigs were slaughtered for food – for cutlets, sausages and other products. In some parts of north-west Germany, there are eight pigs for every person.'

You admit you didn't know that.

'If you care about my advice, London boy, don't become a pork salesman, become what your heart tells you.'

'My heart tells me,' you reply, 'to free all the pigs from all the farms in the world.'

'It's not a bad idea,' says the man. 'About a year ago, I was gripped by the idea of going over to the other side. Joining the activists campaigning to ban or at least reduce the raising of pigs in Germany in insupportable conditions. The older I get, the more it seems to me that we breed living creatures only in order to torture them.'

He reaches across your knee and opens the glove compartment in front of you. He rummages through it and pulls out a business card.

He hands it to you.

It says: *Petra Haidacher, activist, Society Against Cruelty to Animals, Augsburg, Germany.*

There is a telephone number.

The man pulls the business card from your hand, puts it back in the glove compartment and closes it.

'You know what the members of this organisation did?'

You shake your head and ask him to tell you.

You write the answer down in the Book of Lists.

In the middle of the night, they broke into some of the biggest pig farms in Germany and filmed footage that disturbed half the population.

And many people in neighbouring countries.

They filmed a pig that had been trampled on, lying in the alleyway between stalls.

They filmed pregnant sows with bloody wounds on their sides who could not even lie down, let alone turn around, in their narrow cages.

They filmed a wheelbarrow loaded with dead pigs, waiting to be removed.

And much else.

They sent the footage to the organisation Animal Rights Watch, which published it on their website.

The German magazine *Der Spiegel* published an article about what had been filmed and caused a scandal.

The farms sued the activists for illegal entry to their 'animal factories'.

The German court judged that such a break-in was legal if the aim was to show that pig farmers do not take account of EU animal welfare protection measures.

'I didn't know,' you say.

'I meant to join these activists,' said the man. 'Until I remembered that I am soon to retire and that I've got to live off something.'

You turn and look at Ahmed.

He seems to be smiling enigmatically.

29.

What is freedom?

Look through the window.

You're driving through Kočevje, where your family shops, visits the doctor, and goes to the post office or the municipal offices when necessary. Where you used to go to school. Where you were born. And where your father drives to work.

You direct the man on to Ljubljana Street, past the block of flats where you used to live.

'A short-cut,' you explain.

He's surprised you know it, but he says nothing.

The block of flats looks very shabby. In need of renovation. There are some cars parked in front of it. The curtains on the first floor are closed. The tenant lives there. You remember that the flat was very small. Living room, kitchen, bedroom, bathroom.

The standard from Socialist times, your mother once commented bitterly.

We were lucky to have even that, said your father. He was always ready to accept everything that happened to him.

Driving past the flat where you lived for almost fourteen years did not fill you with any feelings. At least, none you could give a name to. The Unfortunate Event robbed you of more than half of what you had inside. The swarm of emotions, hopes and fears, longing, grudges, enthusiasm, disappointment. The content of life.

You see two former schoolmates walking along the pavement opposite. A boy and a girl. You remember their names are Marko and Izabela. They are also a little older, but no different. They don't see you. The car has tinted windows.

And what would they see if they saw you?

A former schoolmate who would never return to his home town? Who had also become, through extreme circumstances, a refugee? And accompanied a refugee from Syria – besides Piggy, your best friend ever – on a long and risky journey across Europe?

You drive on and after a while the man speaks again.

You make a list:

– The production of pigs in Germany is not something its people can be proud of and is sometimes the target of critics from other parts of Europe.

– The farms are big and create a terrible smell, which makes a normal life impossible for residents of nearby villages.

– The stalls contain too many pigs, especially suckling pigs.

– The organisation Animal Rights Watch smuggled cameras into one of the farms owned by Adrianus Straathof and filmed real horrors.

– Including employees killing newly born piglets that seemed too small or weak.

– Or because there were too many and nowhere to put them.

– The video footage clearly showed employees grabbing piglets by the hind leg and smashing them against the floor.

– Some did not die immediately, but shudder in pain for 20 minutes or half an hour.

– Some die by being smothered in droppings that have not been removed when they should have been.

– After seeing the footage, the authorities in Saxony-Anhalt sent a police unit to one of the farms to record all the irregularities and to photograph the many wounded and suffering pigs; they even found out that they were not getting enough water and were dying of thirst.

– The authorities then ordered that the farm be closed down.

– The biggest farm owned by Adrianus Straathof is not far from Berlin, but in various places across Germany he has twenty-five pig farms.

– He has established a true international empire of pig raising, from Netherlands, where he was born, to Belgium, even to Poland, where he is rapidly opening subsidiaries.

– Everywhere, he is in conflict with the local inhabitants.

– Who, however, cannot do without sausages and pork cutlets on their tables.

– 'I'm very unhappy that I have to work for a man who sees pigs only as a source of money,' says the man. 'So, I advise you again,' he turns to you, 'don't even think about selling pork products to supermarkets in Europe.'

'I probably won't,' you reply. 'Almost definitely not. Maybe I'll join Animal Rights Watch. I'll do veterinary studies. So that I can help injured pigs.'

'A smart choice,' says the man.

'But,' you add, 'why do the members of that organisation only get worked up, why don't they do something'

'What can they do?' he asks in surprise.

'They could sneak into the pig farms and free the trapped pigs.'

'My dear boy,' says the man, 'that would be a criminal act. And it's not even possible. Unless you come with cannons and at least a hundred specially trained soldiers. All the farms are heavily guarded. No one who raises pigs can afford to have half his pigs stolen during the night.'

'I don't mean steal them,' you say, 'but to free them from captivity. Help them to go where they want.'

'And where would the millions of pigs freed from farms go? How would they survive? What would they eat? I'm sorry to tell you this, but millions of pigs wandering aimlessly around Europe, looking for something to eat, would cause widespread panic. Who would want to find a pig on their doorstep?'

'I agree,' says Ahmed behind you.

'More and more people think the same about refugees,' adds the man. 'The time will come when they'll start to kill them, as well.'

30.

Ahmed takes the initiative

'Can you stop for a moment, please?' said Ahmed. 'There's a shop I want to go to. I must buy a tin opener. We lost ours and most of our food is in tins.'

Of course, you think. How did you manage to forget that?

'No problem,' says the man and parks near the entrance to the shop. 'Although I was planning to invite you for lunch somewhere on the way.'

'For later,' says Ahmed and gets out.

Then he turns and leans towards you through the back door. 'Can you give me twenty euros? I'm not sure where I put my money.'

You unzip the side pocket on your rucksack, which is between your legs. You take out the envelope with the 2500 euros. You open it and look for a twenty euro note. You don't find one. You take out fifty and hand it to Ahmed, who then heads towards the shop.

You close the envelope and put it away.

'You're not short of money,' says the man, who saw everything.

'Mum and dad said a credit card isn't so handy. It's easier to change cash.'

'That's true,' the man agrees and looks at his watch. 'As I said, I can take you to Frankfurt. Or Munich. Or to anywhere else on the way. I'm glad I picked you up.'

You close the Book of Lists and put it back in your rucksack.

'Diary?' he asks.

'When we get back to London, I have to write a report about our travels. For the school magazine.'

You are telling lies. Do you know what you are doing?

'Can you tell me where all the farms are that Mr Straathof owns in Germany?'

'With difficulty, I don't know them all,' he replies.

'Those you remember.'

But after thinking about it, he says that he only knows the location of two or three. One is in Donauwörth in Bavaria, just after the Austrian border.

'Have you ever been there?'

'Briefly. Three years ago, when the police charged three employees with cruelty to animals. What the result of the prosecution was, I don't know. I only know that they have sows and their young ones there, around eleven thousand.'

'Are there any pig farms were the animals aren't maltreated?'

'I doubt it,' replies the man.

At that moment, Ahmed comes back from the shop and gets into the back seat.

'They searched all the shelves,' he says. 'the assistant said that the usually have them, but they seem to have run out. I hope I didn't keep you waiting too long.'

'It's okay,' says the man.

You drive on and the man is not as talkative as before.

You can feel Ahmed shifting restlessly on the seat behind you. You turn around and see that he has taken off his leather belt and put it on the seat beside him.

'I need the toilet,' he says.

The driver does not notice this. He is lost in thought.

After a while, Ahmed says: 'Can we pull over somewhere? I need to pee.'

The man is silent for a while. Then he says: 'Can you wait a minute? I think there's a filling station soon and I need to get petrol. You'll have enough time to pop to the toilet'

And soon, there appears on the left-hand side a filling station with three pumps and a shop. The man stops at one of the pumps where it says *Diesel*. He gets out and starts to fill the petrol tank.

'Go now,' he says to Ahmed.

But Ahmed is no longer in a hurry.

'I've lost the urge,' he replies.

'You've got an unusual bladder,' says the man.

When he has finished filling the tank, he puts the nozzle back and heads towards the shop.

'I'll go and pay,' he says. 'And to the toilet.'

He turns round and says: 'You should go now, as well, rather than asking me again to stop in ten minutes.'

Ahmed gets out and follows him. The man turns. When he sees Ahmed following him, he points to where the toilets are.

And then he carries on to the shop.

Ahmed suddenly turns, takes a few rapid steps back towards the car and gets into the driver's seat. He turns the key, which the driver left in the ignition, and starts the engine.

He drives off. And you are speeding along the road.

'You stole the car!' you yell.

'Would you rather walk to London?' Ahmed replies.

'But ...'

'Didn't you say we would look for some pig farms on the way and free some pigs? Which means that we shall be stealing someone's property.'

'The police will soon stop us in a stolen car.'

'Don't worry,' says Ahmed, calmly driving towards Ljubljana.

You are lost for words. You expect to hear the howl of a police siren at any moment. Or to be stopped after the next bend by a patrol car. And then, they'll return you to Laze. To mum and dad. Ahmed will be arrested and sent to a refugee centre. His brother will die, and he will never get to London.

You've never been so afraid in your life.

'Look around for a car with German registration,' he tells you.

You look left, right, forward and back, but the only car with a German registration is the one you are in. Only in Ljubljana does luck smile upon you. Ahmed drives into an underground car park in the centre and keeps driving until he sees a white Passat with German registration.

He parks.

He's suddenly in a great hurry. He jumps out, looks around to see if anyone is coming, takes the number plates off the stolen car and shoves them into your hands. The he takes the plates off the Passat and puts them on the ground. He puts the plates from the stolen Mercedes on the Passat and the plates from the Passat on the Mercedes.

'Shall we go?'

You suddenly understand.

If the man with the moustache reports the theft of his car, which he no doubt will, the police will be looking for a black Mercedes. But it will have the number plates from the white Passat, which has the plates from the black Mercedes!

You quickly take the car park ticket to the machine to pay.

Soon after, you are speeding out of the town towards the motorway and not long after, towards Kranj and Jesenice.

'Austria,' says Ahmed. 'First, we need to get to Austria. To a border crossing where there are no checks. Before the Croats took my phone and smashed it, I read that there are now some checks even on the Schengen borders.'

You knew that was right.

'Korensko Sedlo,' you say. 'There's the least traffic there.'

How do you know?

'I went with my parents a few times to Ikea in Klagenfurt. My dad never actually went across Korensko Sedlo, he always used the Ljubelj Pass, but he said that at Korensko Sedlo there were no checks and no queues. You can cross the border without any problems.'

You hope it's still true.

But Ahmed says that hope is no substitute for certainty and so he stops the car on the bend where you can see the border crossing and sends you ahead to see whether it really is easy to get across.

There's no one there. You wave to him and he drives up. Down a road which winds like a snake, you drop into the valley and head towards Villach, without anyone stopping you.

31.
A long way to your goal

In Villach, you park in front of a block of flats that stands on its own. Once again, Ahmed changes the number plates. This time, with a rather scruffy Renault Megane, which also has German registration.

You are amazed that Ahmed knows how to do this. He inserts the long, thin file that he admits he bought in the hardware shop in Kočevje between the window and the frame above the lock on the car door, turns it this way and that, up and down, until there is a click and the door opens.

Then he gets behind the wheel, reaches beneath it, fiddles with something and suddenly the engine starts.

Was he a car thief in Syria?

As he starts the engine, you open the glove compartment of the stolen Mercedes and take out the business card of Petra Haidacher. You put it into your pocket. You have a feeling that it might come in handy.

You put your luggage into the Megane and drive off.

'In case the police are looking for a Mercedes or a Passat,' says Ahmed.

Very crafty, you must admit. You feel safe with Ahmed around. You decide that you will remain his slave. And if not a slave, since that expression is not really appropriate for modern times, his friend.

A friend who you would lie for, if necessary.

But Ahmed, who saved your life, also offered to do something for you.

One-sided friendship does not last long. Ahmed, too, must stick to your agreement.

He said that on the way to London, he would help you free some pigs

That's why you went with him. Mainly that. He promised that on the way, you would free from prison as many pigs as possible and stop the slaughterers cutting their throats. You remind him of the promise. For pigs like your Piggy are clever creatures that deserve to die a natural death.

Like people.

'Like people?' responds Ahmed in an argumentative voice 'Did my thirty relatives die a natural death?'

'Far from it,' you reply.

'Is a pig worth more than a human being?'

You tell him that for you, all living creatures are equal.

'A poisonous spider the same as me?' he looks at you. 'What a high opinion you have of me!'

You explain that he has misunderstood you, that you weren't comparing species, but that it was more the general principle that life is sacred and that we should not take it from anyone violently.

'Then how? Consensually? I'm sorry, Mrs Hen, do you agree that I wring your neck and eat you for dinner?'

It hurts that he is becoming ever more sarcastic. Is he afraid that sooner or later the police will stop you and that it will all be over?

You'd understand that.

You're afraid of that, as well.

But Ahmed is driving very cautiously, never more than 130 km an hour, obeying all the traffic signs, he hasn't committed any offences, even small ones. He is trying to remain unnoticeable among the heavy motorway traffic.

But a police patrol can appear suddenly and without any particular reason. You could fall into a trap set for someone else. If that happens, you wouldn't be able to extricate yourselves.

'Don't be afraid,' says Ahmed after a long silence.

'I'm not,' you say, not quite truthfully.

'I never break a promise that I've made to a friend. We shall free those precious pigs. But first, we must get across the border into Germany.'

'Why? There are pig farms in Austria, too.'

'I'm worried about the Austrian-German border. I know they've set up border controls again at the main crossing. We'll have to find some local border crossing. Once we're in Germany, we can free all the pigs.'

'If we had a map, we could find a small crossing.'

'No one uses maps anymore.'

'The internet!' you exclaim.

'I think I saw one in the wood that we've just driven past,' Ahmed says scornfully.

You resent this. You never expected scorn from him. After all, you're helping him get to London across European countries that he doesn't even know, but they are roughly known to you.

But the sense of resentment doesn't last long, you know he's dependent on you, that he expects the help that you promised him before you set off.

You must find a border crossing into Germany which is so small that only locals use it.

Far from the main roads. Somewhere in the mountains.

In spite of everything, you can't help thinking how much more comfortable Ahmed's journey across Western Europe is compared to what he experienced between Syria and Slovenia, until the moment he pulled you from the river.

You can't help thinking that you deserve at least some of the credit for this.

Although, you don't understand why you weren't smart enough to buy a map of Austria and Germany and France in Ljubljana. You think you made a mistake – you should have realised you'd need a map. Especially considering that you have an old mobile phone with which you can't connect to Google.

That wouldn't have happened before the Unfortunate Event. You would have known exactly what you would need.

On the one hand, you comfort yourself that you haven't had any real difficulties so far, but on the other hand, deep inside, you still secretly hope that something will go seriously wrong and that you'll end up in jail and experience something that will be worth recording in the Book of Lists.

You know that it is wrong to wish this. Because of Ahmed, who is hurrying to London to see his brother before he dies. You'll never forgive yourself if, through your fault, he gets to London too late and you have to visit his brother in the cemetery

While you are wondering where and how to find a small border crossing, you drive past Salzburg. It's not far to the border.

'Turn left at the first opportunity,' you say.

'My fate is in your hands,' says Ahmed.

It's true. That was your agreement. You wrote it in the Book of Lists. 'Help Ahmed get to London, before his brother dies.'

You're doing a bad job.

There's nowhere to turn left. You're on the motorway. Before you have a chance to decide what to do, you find yourselves in a queue of vehicles at the border on the main road from Salzburg to Munich.

There are police in front of you. There are also soldiers, helping the police.

You're stuck. This is where it will end.

Just a few minutes, then you'll never see each other again.

Whose fault is it?

Yours.

32.

Where are the pigs?

Look through the window.

An inner voice keeps telling you to look through the window.

Whose is that voice?

It first appeared after the Unfortunate Event. It's not a voice you can hear, it's more a twitch in your head. You experience it in different ways: as an instruction, as an order. As a request. As advice.

You can never resist it.

This time, too. And so, at the border crossing between Austria and Germany, where you and Ahmed, in a stolen car, are stuck in a long line of vehicles waiting to be checked by armed police, you do as instructed and look through the window.

And what do you see?

Something that brings you great pleasure.

Two police officers are coming down the line of waiting vehicles and excluding the cars with German registration.

They direct you onto another line, where you can drive on without being checked.

Germans trust Germans.

It never occurs to them that in one of the cars with German registration is an underage Slovene and a Syrian refugee, hurrying towards London.

And you're already heading for Munich.

Ahmed's mouth stretches into what in Syria might pass for a smile. And you can't help but give a broad grin.

'Don't celebrate too early,' says Ahmed. 'The hardest part is still ahead of us.'

'Freeing pigs.'

Ahmed says nothing for some time; maybe because you are overtaking a line of cars.

Then he says: 'Do you have a list of pig farms?'

Of course, you don't. And Ahmed knows that only too well. You didn't get one from the German pig salesman, you didn't find one on Google; all you found out was that there are more pig farms in Germany than anywhere and that they are scattered across the country.

You couldn't find data about their location anywhere.

'What now?' asks Ahmed. Are we going to spend a month looking for them? I'm prepared to help you, but I'd hoped you'd have all the data you needed. You surely don't expect me to look? And here in Germany, when I would rather get unnoticed to the French border as soon as possible.'

You feel great sadness.

You didn't expect to see pig farms one after the other along the road, but you hoped they wouldn't be difficult to find. It's true, though, that you didn't think about this very specifically; it was all more a wish than a plan.

You feel like crying.

'I don't know,' you mutter. 'Let's forget the whole thing.'

'Forget it?' Ahmed says in surprise. 'You decide to do something good and then, almost by the by, without any sense of guilt, you say let's forget it. Why? Is it because you are mentally defective or because you are a Christian and that is a characteristic of a faith that is weary of its errors?'

'I'm not a Christian,' you reply. 'But I am mentally defective. Stop the car, I want to get out and go home.'

Ahmed is silent for a long time.

Eventually, he says: 'I can see I'm going to have to think for both of us. Never mind. I promised. And what I promised, I will do. Empty promises are not part of Islam.'

'Nor of Christianity,' you reply.

'I have a different opinion about that,' he says. 'But let's forget that and get down to work. Tell me, where do butchers get the pork that people buy as cutlets for Sunday lunch?'

'From the slaughterhouse,' you say.

'And where does the slaughterhouse get them from'

'From pig farms.' This seems self-evident to you.

'Okay,' says Ahmed, 'shall we make a plan?'

'Let's,' you say, without knowing what he has in mind.

But before you make a plan, you have to promise again not to write anything in the Book of Lists that might connect you in any way with pig farms, just in case the police catch you.

You promise. You swear.

For what feels like the fifth time.

33.

The secret list

Look through the window.

The road signs tell you that you are heading for Stuttgart. You went past Munich five days ago. What have you been doing? The drive from Munich to Stuttgart should take no more than two hours.

Did you have an accident? Did the police catch you, in spite of your caution?

Nothing like that. It's true that on the way, you twice switched cars and swopped number plates, but you also spent your time on an exploit which you may not mention in your Book of Lists.

That is what you promised Ahmed.

But ...

In every life, including yours, sooner or later there appears a 'but'.

You simply didn't want to forget the biggest adventure of your life. You had to write a little. You tried hard to make the sentences as unclear as possible, as ambiguous as possible.

And now the Book of Lists contains things that only you understand.

– Telephone call to Augsburg. Petra Haidacher. Expressions of solidarity, offer of help. Idea of freeing pigs.

– Doubt.

– Return call. Maybe yes. Proposal for a meeting at (name written and then crossed out).

– Ahmed's objections. He's in a hurry to get to London. Persuasion, negotiation, compromise.

– Then agreement.

– Petra and her five activists. They have experience, they know how to sneak into a pig farm at night.

They bring sleeping pills for the dogs and security guards; they bring tools for removing padlocks.

– Without their help, Ahmed and I wouldn't have freed a single pig.

– Driving around Germany from farm to farm, Ahmed is in a hurry, you can only act at night, so you can't visit more than five.

– That's something. In each one there are thousands of pigs.

– The activists sleep in tents, you and Ahmed sleep in the car. In the middle of the day in car parks.

– Night raid. Finally, something happening. You're happy.

– Petra Haidacher is no beauty: thin, anorexic, glasses with thick lenses, a slight limp. But for you, she is the most beautiful girl you've ever seen.

– She is part of the biggest adventure in your life.

– She helps you become a hero. Something that seemed impossible after the Unfortunate Event.

– You realise that you are really a hero when, by chance, you see on the television in a restaurant near the French border a report about how more than twenty thousand pigs are wandering aimlessly around the German countryside. Perhaps twice that number – it's not possible to count them. The sows and their piglets have somehow fled the farms where they were being fattened for slaughter

'Satisfied?' Ahmed asks.

'Not completely,' you acknowledge.

'I've paid my debt,' he says tersely. 'Let's go on.'

34.
A prayer in a mosque

Look through the window.

You're driving through a small town in France. You've stopped writing the names of places in your Book of Lists, there are too many and anyway, you can check your route on the map at any time.

But the building that appears slightly away from the road, on the right, is unusual, different. It's immensely beautiful, almost fairy-tale like.

A mosque.

Ahmed also looks through the window. He puts his foot on the brake and turns into the car park in front of the building.

He switches off the engine. And asks you if you would accompany him inside and pray with him.

You ask him whether, as a Christian, you're allowed to go into a mosque.

Ahmed says that everyone is welcome in mosques, as long as they mean well, even though women have to pray in a different part to men. Which doesn't mean that women don't mean well; but in their vicinity, men may not mean well. For a number of reasons he became more of a theoretical Muslim than a practising one, he doesn't agree with many Muslim customs, but he is convinced that you must honour Allah whenever possible.

Every true Muslim must pray five times a day and most do this at home or out in the open. Mosques are simply temples where people can pray together, affirming mutual connections.

He hasn't been doing this on the way. There has not been the time to kneel five times a day, turn towards Mecca and utter the necessary words. There hasn't been a good opportunity. He didn't want to attract attention and jeopardise the journey to London.

But now he feels that he must make up for having neglected his religious duties with a prayer in a mosque.

Would you join him?

As a thank you for pulling you out of the river and helping you free pigs on the way?

Your last excuse is that you don't know how to pray as a Muslim.

In fact, you don't even know how to pray as a Christian anymore; after the Unfortunate Event and maybe even before it, things like that slipped out of the circle of your attention.

'Just do what I do,' says Ahmed, 'and repeat after me.'

In the middle of the day, the mosque is almost empty. You're in a Muslim temple for the first time and you're astonished by the absence of images that so lavishly and often excessively adorn Christian churches. But the inside still seems extremely beautiful to you, purer, simpler than in Christian churches, in which you've often seen badly executed, amateurish, sometimes almost offensive, images of Jesus Christ.

Before you go in, Ahmed requests that you wash your hands and feet in the stream of water running from a tap into a stone basin in front of the entrance.

You must be clean to pray, he explains, although that was impossible, since you haven't had a shower for a week.

Inside the mosque, Ahmed carries out the following movements, which you copy as accurately as possible:

– Standing, he lifts his arms into the air and says loudly *'Allahu Akbar'*, which means 'God is the greatest'.

– You do the same.

– He folds his arms on his chest and recites the first chapter of the *Quran* in Arabic.

– Since you don't speak Arabic, you can't copy that, so you say only: 'I agree.'

– Ahmed kneels, lifts his arms again and says *'Allahu Akbar'* once more. Then he bows and repeats three times: *'Subhana rabbiyal adheem.'* 'Glory be to my Lord, the Almighty.'

– You repeat this, although your pronunciation of the Arabic phrase is perhaps not the best.

– Ahmed gets up, reciting: *'Sam'i Allahu liman hamidah, Rabbana wa lakal hamd.'* That means 'God hears those who praise Him. Oh our Lord, all praise is to You'.

– You repeat, although not very accurately and perhaps say something else altogether.

– Ahmed lifts his arms once more and says: *'Allahu Akbar.'* Then he drops to his knees, stretches out on the floor and repeats three times: *'Subhana Rabbiyal A'ala.'* He explains that it means: 'Glory be to my Lord, the Most High'.

– You repeat. You kneel, then you stretch out fully with your face turned to the floor.

– Because the phrase is short, you repeat it without mistakes.

– Then Ahmed sits up and repeats: '*Allahu Akbar.*' And again, stretches out with his face down.
– So do you.
– Ahmed rises to his feet and once more says: '*Allahu Akbar.*'
– You copy him.

Then Ahmed says that this was only the first unit of the prayer. You can repeat it twice more, and then you have to recite the first part of the *Tashahhud* in Arabic.

If you go on and do more units – and there is no end to this, you can repeat them endlessly – you have to finish off by reciting the second part of the *Tashahhud*.

At the end, you have to turn right and say: '*Assalamu alaikum wa ramatullah*', which means 'God's peace and blessings be upon you'.

This is how you finished a Muslim prayer in a mosque in a French town, the name of which you don't remember, because you didn't write it in the Book of Lists.

You ask him if he would be willing to do a similar prayer to Jesus in a Christian church. He says no problem, perhaps not gladly, but he owes you this.

But you must first teach him the prayer. In English. You admit it's going to be difficult since you've forgotten the Lord's Prayer and Hail Mary even in Slovene.

You promise to learn both and then teach him. In London, you will visit the most magnificent church in the city and recite both the prayers together.

'And then?' asks Ahmed.

'Then,' you reply, 'your god and my god will become friends. Although I've deserted mine, to be honest. Or he deserted me.'

'That applies to me, too,' says Ahmed.

'Can gods be friends?' you ask.

'Gods are friends,' says Ahmed. 'There can only be one god, although he has a thousand names. Why wouldn't he want to be friends with himself? A bigger question is whether we, people, can be friends.'

'Or people and animals,' you add.

You drive on.

35.
Are pigs your destiny?

Look through the window.

In Northern France, the plain stretching as far as you can see fills you with anxiety, as you are so used to hills. You find it unusual that you've still not been stopped in the stolen car by the police. At the toll booths on the motorway, quite a few other cars were stopped, but you did not seem suspicious to them. Perhaps it helped that the car had German registration plates and that because of the swapped plates no one noticed the stolen car.

But now you're approaching Calais, a port where you won't be able to board a ferry without Ahmed's passport. And you don't have the right documents for the car, either.

What will you do? Swim across the Channel?

A few people have done it, but they were swimmers. Not ordinary swimmers, but exceptional ones.

You are increasingly overcome by a feeling that your journey to London will end on the western shores of France.

'Don't worry,' says Ahmed, as if he has guessed what you're thinking.

When you reach the port of Calais, he joins one of the queues, waiting to board the next ferry. He takes his rucksack out of the boot, tells you to get yours and then he locks the car and sets off for the long line of lorries, also waiting for embarkation.

You feel like he knows what he's doing.

You walk along the endless line of lorries. In some, drivers sit behind the wheel, but most cabins are empty; the drivers know it's going to be a long wait and they're strolling around or drinking beer in the port restaurant.

But Ahmed is not paying attention to the cabins, instead he's checking the back doors. They are mostly closed, and the trailers have metal walls so that it's impossible to see what they're transporting. The two of you move from one lorry to the next.

You're not the only ones, many people are walking around the port or rushing to and fro; you don't stand out in any way and no one is paying you any attention. You give the impression of being two passengers, awaiting embarkation. And you are. And you would be two of the many, if Ahmed had a passport.

But because he hasn't got one, you have to improvise.

And Ahmed improvises.

Just as well, because you wouldn't know what to do.

Among the lorries that are not closed off with metal walls or canvas, you find one that has a trailer covered with wide wooden boards that 'breathe'; through the gaps between them you can see the cargo. You can't believe it: inside there are pigs, packed closely together, on three levels. It seems they're asleep, they're not moving or making a sound. They're waiting to be exported to Great Britain where, without a doubt, they'll be slaughtered and served as roasts in fancy restaurants or at private parties of rich English people.

Your instinct tells you that you and Ahmed should open the back door and let them out.

But Ahmed has a different idea.

You won't free the pigs. You'll join them in captivity.

As the pigs cannot escape and as it's unlikely that anyone would want to steal them, the back door isn't locked, just closed with a bolt that can easily be lifted.

And with the door opened.

You can climb inside.

And that's what you do. You open the door, climb into the lorry and onto the middle level. Then you pull the door to, reach out through the gap, and replace the bolt so that it holds the door closed. The pigs are crammed in so tightly that you find it quite difficult to make your way to the front of the trailer; it is clear not just to Ahmed but also to you that here you will be least visible from outside.

Your incursion into their temporary home disturbs the pigs, they start grunting and squealing. But not for long. When they see that you're not dangerous, they calm down. Especially when you two, thirsty as you are, drink some water from the basin at the front.

There's also a trough with food, where the biggest and most selfish pigs are shoving each other. The pressure on you is so great that after a while you start finding it difficult to breathe.

'*Allahu akbar.*' Ahmed gives thanks for your luck.

What would you do if none of the lorries in the endless line was transporting pigs? You couldn't have hidden in any other lorry. Except with the driver's agreement. It seems unlikely to you that any of them would want to smuggle two

153

refugees into Britain. And how lucky that the driver wasn't in the lorry with the pigs but had probably gone for a drink during the wait.

Did Allah really ensure that you were lucky?

'Soon we'll be at your brother's,' you try to reassure Ahmed.

But Ahmed sees it differently. The greatest problems are still ahead of you. At least a hundred things can go wrong. When the driver comes back, he may look inside and see you. Or notice one of your rucksacks, which the pigs can't conceal completely. If he doesn't suspect anything and drives onto the ferry, then goes to the restaurant onboard, since no one is allowed to stay in a parked vehicle, you'll be trapped for an hour and a half among the pigs that will piss and shit on you.

Which is what they're doing already.

Can you last?

And what happens at the other side?

The lorry has a German registration plate, so it won't be subject to customs checks. But almost certainly someone on the British side is bound to check the cargo coming across the Channel, at least some vehicles if not all, and with imports of animals some papers, declarations or something like that surely have to be signed. Above all, the driver will have to show his passport at passport control. The possibility of being discovered is a hundred times greater than the chance that you'll remain hidden until reaching your destination.

What destination? You don't know that, either.

What if the lorry was bound for Birmingham, Salisbury or even Bristol? How and where will you sneak out? How, covered in piss and shit, will you reach London? Where will you clean up? Even just at a glance you'll seem extremely suspicious.

Just one encounter with the police and it's all over.

'Let's be prepared for the worst,' says Ahmed.

36.
Can gods be friends?

But you, for the first time, feel that all will be well. You're convinced that the whole world population of pigs is on your side. Maybe pigs also have their gods, like people, and maybe those gods made sure that right at the start of your journey you came across a talkative pig seller, who gave you so much interesting and useful information.

And the fact that before crossing the Channel, you were able to hide in a lorry transporting pigs? One coincidence is possible, two are less likely, but three coincidences on a single journey can only be the will of higher forces. And anyway, as Ahmed says, there are no coincidences, only fate. And perhaps Allah is mainly looking after Ahmed, making sure he gets to his brother's. And looking after you because you are helping him.

You become aware that it isn't appropriate to think things like this in a crowd of pigs, covered in pig urine and excrement from head to toe.

'What are you thinking about?' asks Ahmed while you're waiting to board the ferry.

'About a just world,' you reply. 'About god's world.'

'I've got to tell you something,' he says. 'Of all the people I've met in my life, you're the most unusual by far. I'd never imagined there were such people.'

'Really?'

'Maybe you don't know, but what followed the Unfortunate Event, is god's gift. Everyone should experience the world as a nightmare, as something that has strayed from the right path, but in a kind way, with patience and hope.'

'Like me?'

'You possess all that in a hugely greater amount than me. It's an honour for me that we're friends. Allah himself put you in my path. He's got plans for both of us. I increasingly believe that we'll get to London without any problems.'

'So do I,' you say. 'It seems that my Christian god wants that, too. Maybe I'll become Christian again.'

'But that's what you already are,' says Ahmed. 'You were born a Christian. The period without faith was only a deviation. Like when picking mushrooms, you stray onto a path where mushrooms don't grow. Sooner or later you'll see them again.'

'Do mushrooms grow in Syria, too?'

'Can I tell you something?' asks Ahmed. 'It seems to me you're incarcerated. That you live between the walls of a small room, as if in prison. And that the walls of that prison are what prevents you from seeing the wider picture. Ideas that you cannot reconcile with different ones. Look through the window sometimes. You'll see that the world out there is different.'

'That's it!' you reply. 'All the time I hear inside me a voice telling me: Look through the window! I don't know where it's coming from. And I look. Not always, but I often look through the window. But I don't often see something I haven't seen before. And first, I have to come to the window. The right one. You know that windows differ. So far, I've not found one through which to see something new.'

'You shouldn't take the instruction to look through the window literally,' says Ahmed. 'It's a different window and a different look.'

'I don't understand.'

'You will sooner or later,' says Ahmed.

37.

Across the Channel

Look through the window.

You're in London. Not quite in London, but in a place called East Molesey, one of the outer suburbs, you could say – even though officially it lies in Surrey – near Hampton Court Palace, on the fifth floor of a block of flats called Thames Court.

From the balcony, you can see the River Thames flowing past.

You're on your own, Ahmed and his brother Imran have gone into the city.

You're writing in your Book of Lists about the events on the journey from the port of Calais in France to where you are now.

Even though Ahmed said you had to be prepared for the worst, the journey to London went without serious complications. No one stopped, arrested, questioned or imprisoned you. The latter was what Ahmed feared the most, since his brother would die before Ahmed saw him for the last time.

And your journey would have been in vain.

At first, there were no problems.

The hefty, bald, German-looking lorry driver came back to his vehicle and walked around it, peering in here and there to check if the pigs were alright. He didn't seem to be doing this very carefully, just out of habit. Then he climbed behind the wheel, which made the front of the lorry sway slightly because of his weight and turned on the engine. The sound disturbed the pigs who responded with gentle grunts and squeals.

But they soon stopped, knowing that nothing special was happening.

The lorry moved, the driver followed the vehicles in front, at a metal booth he showed his passport and some other papers, and then slowly drove on and followed the instructions of the port employees waving their arms and directing him onto the ferry, where other lorries already stood at the sides and in front of him, so he had to stop. Another lorry stopped immediately behind him and then the next.

The loading went quickly and smoothly, all the drivers were used to the procedure.

The lorry driver climbed out of his cabin, slammed the door without locking it, blew his nose several times into a handkerchief, which he then carefully folded and put in his pocket. He set off for the stairs that led up to the deck. All the other drivers did the same; no one was allowed to stay in their vehicle during the crossing.

'What do you think,' whispered Ahmed after you were left alone and the last of the three employees who had directed and supervised the parking were gone, 'will they lock the door or leave it unlocked?'

What does it matter, you asked.

'If they don't lock it, we can sneak to the nearest toilet and get some water.' He shook the two empty plastic bottles that lay between us. You were both very thirsty. How stupid not to have bought some water in the shop in the port. But you were too busy thinking about finding a suitable lorry.

You didn't dare take a risk, you stayed among the pigs and drank the water from their trough.

One of the pigs, the one pressed against you in the crowd, had been staring into your eyes with great interest from the very beginning. As if unable to look anywhere else. As if seeing something familiar there. It reminded you of your Piggy, when he was little.

Did he sense the affection you'd felt for your murdered friend?

You stroked his back a few times and every time he grunted gently with pleasure.

At the same moment, something else happened. When you looked at the other pigs, squashed into the lorry, you suddenly realised they weren't all the same, as we usually think, but each one had slightly different features, different eyes, a different snout; in short, they were all individuals. Even though they were unable to express their individuality clearly enough for people to notice.

Maybe animals have a soul, too, you thought. Maybe each one is unhappy about his fate in his own way. They were definitely unhappy. Especially the one persistently staring into your eyes. Most of the others turned their feelings of fear and anxiety into apparent indifference.

Suddenly, it no longer seemed unusual to you that you'd found your best friend among pigs. Although during the journey, Ahmed was also becoming your friend, a very good one. But friendships among people are self-evident.

Although not necessarily between Christians and Muslims.

You felt the ferry shake and start to move. It swayed, although not much. The sea was obviously not too choppy. You knew that it took an hour and a half from Calais to Dover.

Although you were afraid that after you arrived the worst would happen and you would end up in the hands of the British police, which would end worse for Ahmed as a refugee without a passport – you, as a European Union citizen, would manage to wriggle your way out somehow – someone ensured that everything went smoothly.

Allah, God or the pigs' god?

After landing, the driver, who had returned from the deck, turned on the engine as soon as he got behind the wheel and drove off the ferry when it was his turn, without checking whether all his pigs were still there. Clearly, he had done this journey a thousand times already. He showed some papers to the British police. *Immigration*, it said above the door of the metal booth, in which the police officers checked the documents. Then the driver calmly, without any panic, drove on, meandering around Dover until he got to the motorway for London.

For the second time on this journey you experienced the absence of any complication, not even a small one, as an injustice. Your journey to London was an adventure and if everything went without problems, the adventure was less interesting, less than ones you'd seen on television, in any case. One way or another, it seemed wrong to you. For the first time in your life, you were experiencing something unusual, something more important than your walk to school and back home again.

Without daring to admit it, you really wished that something would go wrong.

161

During the drive to London, you didn't know that the biggest complications were still ahead. You knew even less that things would go their own way without you being able to influence them.

And that in the end you would find out that your story, maybe every human story, belongs to Fate and much less to you. And that, above all else, we're all victims.

Although victims of the wrong decisions rather than events.

38.

Filthy tourists

During the drive to London, the German driver stopped at a petrol station. He got some fuel, then locked the cabin and went to the nearby restaurant. It was three o'clock in the afternoon. He was obviously hungry.

You were hungry, too. And Ahmed. You'd run out of tins.

The pigs were also hungry, as they had eaten everything in their troughs.

But Ahmed said you must wait till the end of the journey. If the driver was not going to London, which was unlikely, but to a pig farm somewhere around London or, god forbid, in the north of England or even in Wales or Scotland, you would have to find an opportunity to escape from the lorry before it reached its destination.

But it was too early for an escape. Filthy as you were, it would be difficult to get to London. You were forced to follow the lorry's direction and decide as you went along.

That's what Ahmed said.

During the drive to London, next to the piggy that was pressed against you, staring at you in the hope that you would maybe save it from captivity, you suddenly remembered that it would be wise to turn on your mobile phone, which had been turned off throughout your journey through Germany and France. Just in case.

Maybe mum and dad had sent you at least one text.

But Ahmed – not for the first time – reminded you that using your mobile could be dangerous. The American National Security Agency monitors all internet and mobile communications in the world.

What would you do if they caught him and put him in prison?

The driver came back happy and full, he did a quick round of the lorry to see if the pigs were alright, checked the bolt on the back door and then drove on.

Ahmed said that you would have to sneak off the lorry before it reached London. Even if the driver wasn't planning on stopping there but would drive on, god knows where, maybe to Wales or Cornwall. You couldn't know. But your destination was London, so you'd have to get off at the right moment and in the right place. Or, if necessary, jump off. Move closer to the back door and wait for the lorry to stop at a red light. Lift the bolt, push the door and jump onto the road. And then into the nearest bushes.

Risky, he said. But you had no other choice.

You did have another choice.

Perhaps not a choice, but Fate gave you an opportunity that was not among the worst scenarios.

Near London, the driver turned on to the southern ring road and Ahmed, who said he had looked several times at a map of Greater London on Google when he was still in Syria, expressed his fear that the driver was perhaps delivering pigs to one of the pig farms in the west of England, maybe even in Cornwall.

During the Channel crossing, he had realised something that you, to your shame, had not: that all the pigs were female and that they were probably being driven to a farm, where sows are kept for breeding. This was really the most plausible explanation, as it didn't make sense to transport ordinary pigs from Germany to England.

There was no other option but to wait. Ahmed at least knew that you needed to escape while the lorry was still on the M25 motorway and before it turned on to the M3, leading westwards.

Soon after the turning for Aldershot, the lorry drove to a large service area, and parked among the other lorries; the driver locked the cabin and went to the shop at the other side of the petrol station.

'Let's go,' said Ahmed. With one last look into her eyes, you said goodbye to the piggy and, with your rucksack, pushed behind Ahmed toward the back door. He lifted the bolt from inside and you both jumped out. Ahmed closed the door, pushed the bolt back in its place and set off for the shop and the restaurant.

'Toilets,' he kept repeating, 'we must find the toilets.'

When he was about ten metres away, you quickly lifted the bolt and opened the door wide. The pigs gave you a surprised look. None of them moved. Sooner or later they would, you thought, and hurried after Ahmed.

The people getting out of their parked cars or returning to them were giving you strange looks. You were covered in pig shit from head to toe. As were your rucksacks. Many probably thought you had fallen into a cesspit or a ditch, although there were no signs of it having rained recently.

But Ahmed, much more experienced than you, maybe because of the tragedies he had experienced, or because he wasn't mentally damaged like you, soon found a way to the toilets. He told you to clean yourself up with paper and water as much as possible; he did the same. The smell, of course, remained. Then, wet through, but with clean faces, you went back outside.

Ahmed suddenly ran to a taxi that was getting petrol next to one of the pumps. And you followed. The taxi driver couldn't have given you a more surprised look, even though he was trying to hide it. But he didn't object when Ahmed asked him to take you to Hampton Court Palace.

'You can't be tourists,' the taxi driver said.

'We are,' said Ahmed, offering him fifty euros from the money you had stolen from your mum.

'Pounds, pounds,' insisted the taxi driver who, judging by his appearance, came from the Near East. Ahmed spoke Arabic to him.

You didn't understand what he told him, but everything was soon sorted.

He drove you to Hampton Court. There, Ahmed spoke Arabic to him again and he took you to a Tesco supermarket in East Molesey. There, Ahmed gave him more euros. The taxi driver was satisfied, he hadn't turned on the meter during the drive.

Then, as if he knew exactly where you were, Ahmed took you past the shop to the street behind it. And then left, and right, and you were in front of a quite tall block of flats by the Thames.

Thames Court. You took the lift to the fifth floor.

And rang the bell.

The door was opened by Imran, Ahmed's older brother.

Who didn't look at all ill.

Evidently, he had got better since Ahmed last talked to him.

39.

What is happening?

Look through the window.
Something is not right. Increasingly you feel that something isn't as you expected. Although that's quite normal and you're used to the feeling, after your arrival in London you've been full of uncertainty and worry.
And anxiety.
The view you see is of the south-western part of the city, the outer suburbs of East and West Molesey. Past the block, on the right, flows the Thames. You vaguely remember that when you, mum and dad visited London with a tourist agency, many years back, you only saw the sights in the centre, and you didn't even imagine that the city had suburbs.
And now you're here. In a small flat that Ahmed's older brother Imran rents from a friend, called Morris; that's what it says on the door and under the bell at the entrance to the block of flats and on the post box. Surprisingly, Imran's English is worse than Ahmed's, although evidently, he's been living in London for quite some time. They don't resemble

each other, either. Sometimes you feel that maybe they're not brothers at all. But brothers don't always look alike.

The flat is small, but you have your own bedroom, with a bed that needs to be lifted during the day and pushed into a space in the wall. Ahmed and Imran sleep in a bigger bedroom, in which they spend a lot of time, even during the day, talking about something or other, in Arabic, of course, which you don't understand.

You have a feeling that Ahmed is neglecting you slightly. But that seems normal; he and his brother have a lot to say to each other.

The flat is not very tidy, there's hardly anything in the kitchen except eggs and dry bread and fruit juice; this is what you have for breakfast every day. But you are glad of the bathroom, shower, soap, towels; after a long time, your body is clean again. It's no longer unpleasant and alien, like it was on the last leg of the journey to London.

You find it unusual that there's no television in the flat.

Or computer.

Or phone.

You find it unusual that Ahmed, whose phone was evidently smashed on the border by the Croatian police, has not bought a new one immediately after your arrival in London. Maybe Imran gave him a new one. But neither of them uses a phone in the living room. Always only in their bedroom. To where they often retreat, even during the day. They keep talking to someone.

You find it unusual that every time they go to their bedroom, they lock the door.

As if they're afraid of something.

Imran doesn't cook and for the first three days you don't leave the flat; every day around midday, an elderly Arab with a turban brings you bags of food, which Ahmed says is

Lebanese and is called *meze*. You like it. While you all eat at a round table in the living room, Ahmed and Imran are silent, deep in thought, only Ahmed occasionally remembers that you're there and asks if you've ever eaten anything better.

And every time, you reply politely that you haven't.

'We're taking you to a Lebanese restaurant tomorrow,' says Ahmed during a late lunch on the third day.

'I've spent all my money,' you say.

'I know,' says Ahmed. 'On me. But you're our guest here.'

'That's right,' says Imran in his bad English. But his face remains gloomy. Ever since you and Ahmed arrived, he hasn't smiled once. As if he's very worried about something. As if a dark cloud lay on top of him. Which you find understandable. He probably found out from Ahmed about the massacre of their relatives. You've only lost Piggy, they've lost their whole family.

You're surprised they want to go on living at all.

But their will to live is more than obvious. The next day you're joined in the Lebanese restaurant by three young Arabs, probably Syrians, but their conversation at the table, from which you are excluded, becomes very lively at times, almost on the verge of an argument, and then it calms down again and often turns into whispers.

After a while, you gather courage to ask Ahmed what they're talking about.

'About us,' says Ahmed, without hesitation. 'We're both here illegally, I without a passport, you without an entry stamp and, as a minor, without your parents' permission. We're talking about how to legalise our stay here.'

'If I'm in the way, I can go back home.'

'Don't talk nonsense,' says Ahmed. 'We're your friends, we need you.'

Then he explains something in Arabic to the others. Probably something Imran has already heard, but the other three have not. One of them, the one sitting on your right, pats you on your shoulder. The other two nod approvingly; one even smiles.

'I told them how we freed the pigs in Germany,' says Ahmed. 'But now allow us to discuss how to legalise our stay. Unless you'd rather go home.'

'Not for the time being,' your reply earnestly.

After all, Ahmed is your best friend. You have to continue taking care of him. To serve him. Like you promised. You're certain that sooner or later he will tell you what he wants from you.

40.

Do animals have a soul?

Look through the window.

There's an unusual cloud above London. A mixture of smoke and fog, something dark, even frightening. Is there a storm coming? No, it's not a normal cloud, it has too many shades of sadness in it. It's suffused through and through with gloominess.

You're recording in the Book of Lists one of your last conversations with Ahmed.

Never before has he found it unusual that your best friend was a pig. After all, many people get attached to dogs, cats, hamsters, parrots and other animals, he said. He also understood that after Piggy's death, especially because you ate his blood without knowing, you suffered greatly.

And that you experienced the manner of his death as an injustice.

You were grateful to Ahmed for his compassion, and this gratitude was the foundation of your relationship. Even more than your gratitude to him for saving your life.

But now, a week after your arrival in London, he's suddenly changed his opinion. Now he claims that a friendship between an animal and a person is not possible, because there are too many differences between them.
You're surprised.
You ask him to list the differences.
You write down the list.
– Although we have a lot in common with animals, particularly some of them, and although we are all aware of the world around us and our place in it, and although animals feel pain, fear, hatred, even love for their offspring and try to protect them at all cost, and although some animals even have memory, they don't have something important.
– Imagination. They aren't capable of turning what they are aware of into a story, which would tell or explain something to them, and which would also mean something to other animals of their kind. And because they lack this ability they don't know where they're coming from, why they're here or what is the purpose of their life.
– Animals don't have a soul.
– People do.
– And that's important. Even if we neglect all the other human characteristics.
– Has a pig ever written a good book? Or come up with a fairy tale to entertain its young ones in the evening? Has a pig ever painted anything that was exhibited in a national gallery? Or discovered electricity, invented a steam engine or a rocket with which to fly to the moon? Has a pig invented a mobile phone or a computer?
– Will a pig be the one to develop technology to the extent that computers and robots may soon become cleverer than us?
– What does a pig know about the origin of the world and life, or about god, religion and religious duties?

– Nothing. Because pigs don't have a soul.
– It's natural that animals serve man and not the other way round. Animals are here for us to use, or at least some of them, for higher, human goals because people, let's be honest, are superior beings, divine beings, even though we don't know how to be human to each other.
– Human bloodthirstiness is not God's work, but Satan's. That's the problem of the world we are living in. Satan has moved into our hearts, souls and heads; we don't even know anymore what is God's and what is his. He has confused us.
– But while we stay faithful to God, while we respect his commandments, our soul will remain his, pure and divine. Even if we have to kill our enemies for this.

41.

We don't get offended by our friends

As you're writing all this down in the Book of Lists, you have a lump in your throat and tears are running down your cheeks.

What has happened to Ahmed? He didn't think like this before. Has he been poisoned in some way at the mosque he goes to every day since your arrival in London, has he been brainwashed or had a chip inserted in his head?

Although it's true that you didn't discuss things like this on the journey and that he has maybe always thought like this.

But no, you did talk about religion, about what a disaster it is for humankind that there are so many different gods and religions and religious sects, who kill each other; he himself said that the greatest disaster for Islam was the split between the Sunnis and Shiites, who don't kill each other any less bloodthirstily than they are both killed by Christians.

Saudi planes bombed a hospital in Yemen, killing over fifty innocent Muslim children; is that a smaller sin than the

American, Russian, British, French and even Syrian planes killing an infinite number of his fellow countrymen?

Among them thirty of his relatives?

Was what the Islamic State did God's work, had Allah told them to do it? Ahmed agreed that he had not. He agreed with you that it would be easier to find a needle in a haystack than a person with pure and sincere faith, without elements of human weakness.

When you said that this is why you're an atheist, for if God really did exist, he would not allow such things, or all the other wars and massacres throughout history, Ahmed said nothing and no longer wanted to talk.

In fact, he never wanted to talk to you about things like that. Only once, in the middle of the night, when you were lying in a field somewhere in Germany, staring at the starry sky, did the conversation turn to god and religion.

The conversation is written in your Book of Lists.

He asked you if you were aware of:

– the infinite nature of the universe,
– black holes,
– stars that explode and become supernova,
– the speed with which constellations are moving away from the invisible centre, the point of the Big Bang, the alleged beginning of everything that is.

You also wrote down your replies:

– that you had not talked about this at school yet, at least not in detail,
– but you had seen a few programmes about it on the National Geographic channel,
– but before the Unfortunate Event,
– because after it, you no longer understood many things,
– and above all, neither before nor later had you found a connection between the universe and religion. And you can't find one now.

Look at the stars, said Ahmed. Can you imagine all this wondrous infinity appearing out of nothing? And that the laws regulating all this, the laws of physics, created themselves? And that there's no higher force maintaining balance and directing events in the universe?

You replied that you do find the universe magnificent and frightening at the same time,

– and that there are more things in the world than a hundred Einsteins could understand,

– and that a god maintaining and controlling it all does not bother you,

– what bothers you is the excessive number of religions that are in conflict with each other,

– and which throughout history have brought humankind more misery than good and continue to do so.

After all, if there is a god, there can only be one.

So why, according to the data you found online, are there over 4200 different religions? Forms of worship? Commandments about what is right and what isn't?

Why would God, if he created everything, including religions, deliberately create confusion?

Ahmed tells you that you can find the answer to this in the *Quran*.

God created different religions in order to test us.

The *Quran* says: 'We have appointed a law and a practice for every one of you. Had God willed, He would have made you a single community, but He wanted to test you regarding what has come to you. So compete with each other in doing good. Every one of you will return to God and He will inform you regarding the things about which you differed.'

You admit this sounds nice and may be convincing enough for many people.

But for you, it does not reach deep enough to dispel the doubts and direct you back to religion, which spontaneously evaporated from you like steam when you turned twelve and started using the computer a lot, browsing the internet, acquainting yourself with a myriad of different views, finding out how true it is that almost no one is completely right and how foolish it is to cling to one opinion only.

And if god existed, he would count it in your favour that on the way to London you freed some pigs. Would God, or Allah, if he really is just, not find in this a sufficient reason to forgive everything bad that you had done in your life? Although with regard to yourself, you can't really remember having done anything really bad and with regard to Ahmed, you can't imagine him doing anything bad.

Don't get offended, says Ahmed, if after all that we've been through together and in spite of your selfless help on my journey to London, where I've been sent by Fate, and in spite of the friendship that has grown between us, for we really are better and more honest friends than most people in this world, don't get offended if I tell you a truth that may hurt you. I don't want our friendship to end now, when I need it the most.

You assure him that it won't.

With the exception of Piggy, murdered by your parents, you have never had a better friend than Ahmed.

He could get offended by you comparing him to a pig. He could convince you that your mum and dad wanted to make you happy with your birthday present because they simply didn't know how much Piggy meant to you, so you can't really blame them for it.

But we don't get offended by our friends, he adds.

We try to understand them.

In spite of this, he wants to tell you that your freeing of pigs on your journey through Germany will not produce the results you had in mind. Most of the pigs that you 'freed', which were actually chased out, have already been caught by the farmers and returned to where they lived before.

A lot of the pigs, perhaps half, returned to their sties on the farms voluntarily, because they didn't know what to do after being 'freed'. They missed regular meals, they were scared of dogs and people and traffic, scared of the world they weren't used to.

Since Piggy was your friend, you probably know that, in spite of the differences, there are many similarities between people and pigs. Many prisoners, after finding themselves free after forty years in prison, don't do well outside, don't know what to do with themselves. Some hang themselves. Others commit the first crime that enters their head, so that they can return to prison as soon as possible. Back to the environment where everything is clear to them and they don't have to worry about where their next meal is coming from.

Why would pigs be any different?

He's sorry, he says, that he has to tell you this, but with your 'liberation' you made most of the pigs unhappy rather than happy. Non-Muslims keep pigs in order to eat them sooner or later, either roast on a barbecue or processed into various meat products.

There's nothing wrong with this. People live on food.

Muslims don't eat pigs, Hindus don't eat beef.

But this doesn't change the fact that all living beings need food.

The last thing he wants is to offend you, but it seems right to him that you don't have too many illusions about your heroic acts. It was nice, interesting and exciting.

But now it's time for another story.

'No,' you say. 'We'll go on freeing pigs in England. I can't believe that they are better off in pigsties than outside. You've got to help me. You promised.'

Ahmed says nothing for a while, but stares through the window.

Sad? Confused? Angry?

'Before setting off, you told me something that I will now repeat in a slightly different way,' you say. 'Don't befriend a pig farmer if you don't have room for his pig.'

The expression on Ahmed's face relaxes into a smile.

'We have a deal,' you say.

'It's true. Each of us carries a burden we can't offload. That's why we made a deal for me to help you and you to help me. I've helped you. Now it's your turn. Now you have to help me. Only then we can free pigs again.'

You realise he's right. You promised to serve him.

Not just that, you promised to be his slave.

Now he's the one needing help.

'What do you expect from me?'

Nothing special, he says. You'll have to do a few errands. A few tasks. This and that. Nothing forbidden, nothing that would get you into trouble.

But you mustn't say a word to anyone.

Can he rely on you?

He can, you reply. Surprised.

Is he doubting the friendship that has never been questionable?

That this is perhaps the case you sense when, just before setting off into the city with his brother, he gives you a hug. On your journey to London, you hugged at least once a day and every time you felt that the hug was a thank you for a successful day and a sincere confirmation of your friendship.

But now, for the first time you feel his hug doesn't come from his heart.

Something is bothering him. He has doubts.

'Don't you wonder,' he says, 'that our journey, mainly yours, is connected with pigs?'

'Should I?'

'Of course! Because your parents killed your friend, you wanted to drown in the river. Because I got there at the right moment, I saved you. Is that a coincidence? We set off on a journey, hitchhiked, and we were picked up by a pig salesman. He gave us lots of information about pig farms in Germany. Is that a coincidence? Even the contact for the activists that helped you free tens of thousands, perhaps hundreds of thousands of pigs, came from him. Is that a coincidence? We smuggled ourselves into England on a lorry, transporting pigs. It could be transporting anything, but it was transporting pigs. Is that a coincidence, too?'

'I don't know,' you say with a shrug.

Scared.

'You think it means something?' you ask him.

'You think it's all coincidence?'

'What else could it be?'

'Fate?'

'I don't believe anything like that exists,' you say.

You really don't.

'So what would you call what has happened to you so far? A sequence of coincidences, no more?'

'I don't know. Do you have a better answer?'

'The only right answer is Fate,' says Ahmed. 'Which is at the same time a sequence of coincidences, ordered by Allah.'

'I don't get it,' you admit.

Although in your current state you're willing to believe anything anybody tells you.

'Allah,' says Ahmed, 'or God, as you call him, determines the fate of each of us at birth. He writes it in the Book of Lists, where each of us in our own way writes the realisation of the fate determined for us. Only Allah knows what a sequence of events means in our life. All we can do is choose among the tasks he sets before us. The results are not up to us. The results can be events that aren't connected, or a sequence of events originating from each other. The fate of the sequential encounters with pigs and your dependence on them was determined by Allah. Because he realised that a pig as a living being resides in the heart of your soul.'

You're silent for a very long time.

Finally, you say: 'I'd like to object. But don't know how. I live my fate. And that's enough for me.'

'For me, too,' says Ahmed.

42.

Driving around London

Look through the window.

You're alone in the flat again. You feel deserted. There's no computer, so you can't browse the internet. You've got your mobile phone, but who can you call? There are moments when you want to call dad, but you change your mind each time.

You're abroad. And abroad, things aren't as you think they should be.

If your money wasn't all gone you could take a bus or the underground to go around London and look at the sights. You could ask Ahmed to lend you some money, but you don't want to. Maybe he's penniless, too. And dependent on his brother.

You're not happy, but you try to put up with it. You look through your Book of Lists, reading bits here and there.

This is your life.

'You' are the sum of your notes. Plus a few memories, which often seem like the result of your imagination.

And then Ahmed invites you on a tour of London. Imran would like to come, too, but he doesn't have the time.

First, you look at Hampton Court, where the infamous Henry VIII lived. You're slightly worried because his story doesn't interest you at all, but that's how it is. The anxiety you feel is stronger.

From there, you go into the centre and walk around Oxford Street. So many shops! And nothing you can afford to buy. Ahmed says that this is the main characteristic of the West: everything is expensive, too expensive.

'But,' he says, 'we don't need anything.'

You agree.

At this moment all you need is a little hope, a little trust in the future, a little peace in your soul, less fear that something is happening that you will not cope with. But you can't tell Ahmed that.

It's all foreign to him, as well. But it doesn't seem to unsettle him.

When you repeat and emphasise that you don't want to go into any of the shops, he suggests you have a look at London from the top floor of a double decker. Since you're in London, you have to have a look at it. And you ride around on buses from ten in the morning till seven in the evening. All over the place. There's hardly a bus you don't get on and then off again and take another one.

'Can you remember the numbers of these buses?' asks Ahmed.

The question is a strange one, since you write them down as you go along in your Book of Lists, which you always carry with you.

'You can continue tomorrow,' he says when you get tired.

He gives you an Oyster Card, which you can use to travel on the underground or buses. He also has one, but he had to pay for both of them.

Where did he get the money? Definitely not from his brother.

You're grateful to him. Now you can go sightseeing whenever you want.

Although, after a day of riding on buses you're so tired that it's the last thing you want to do.

But the very next day Ahmed asks you to take a small rucksack to a Syrian, a friend of his dad's. He'll meet you at Victoria Railway Station. You'll have to take quite a few buses. You don't have to look for the man you must give the rucksack to, he'll recognise you. He'll wait for you under the arrivals and departures board. Give him the rucksack and take the same route home to Thames Court.

In case there's no one at home, he gives you the keys to both entrance doors.

'Although my brother and I are bound to be here,' he says.

43.

Something goes wrong

Look through the window.

You're riding on a double decker bus along Bayswater Road past Hyde Park on your right. You're sitting upstairs, at the front, which you like as you can see everything that's happening in front of the bus. Although nothing dramatic is happening. Some cars are turning left into Edgeware Road, some right into Park Lane, while the rest carry straight on to Oxford Street.

The bus keeps stopping, people get on and off. At the end of Hyde Park, the bus turns right, into Park Lane. And then towards Victoria Station. The rucksack is between your legs. Next to you sits an American tourist, a corpulent gentleman, whose weight is pressing you into the corner. He's talking to his wife and daughter, sitting on the seats to the right.

You find it strange that the rucksack is locked with a padlock, but Ahmed must know what he's sending to the man at Victoria, whom you don't have to recognise because he will recognise you. You don't want to know what's in it. It's rather heavy, so you assume it contains Arabic books or a computer, one of those on which you can access Google and email in Arabic.

After all, this is what has been confusing you so far: that Imran didn't have a computer. Maybe he's had it all along but hasn't used it because it wasn't working. Whoever is waiting for you at Victoria, will probably fix it. That's why you're delivering it to him.

Maybe then you'll also have access to Gmail and Google.

And you'll get in touch with dad.

Will you ever return home?

What you really want to do is stay in London and leave your fate to Ahmed. You're certain that sooner or later he'll take care of you. One way or another. You trust him. After the prayer in France, you feel you're not just friends but also brothers.

How would a brother not take care of a brother?

Together you've liberated tens of thousands of pigs!

But in the large terminal of Victoria Station, you get confused. In the middle of the crowd that is bigger than you expected, as it's five in the afternoon, when people leave work, no one recognises you. You first stand in one open place, then in another, then in yet another and yet another. Everyone is rushing to catch a train home.

For over an hour and a half you move around the enormous space, standing in exposed spots in the hope that someone will recognise you, come to you, take the rucksack and enable you to return to Thames Court.

Nobody comes.

If Ahmed had a mobile, you could call him and ask what's gone wrong. Obviously, there's been some misunderstanding.

As it is, you don't know what to do.

This is why you take the same buses to return home with the rucksack, to East Molesey, to Thames Court by the Thames. On the way from the bus stop to the block of flats, you feel tempted to find out what's in the rucksack. You put it on the ground and feel it on all sides. It seems there's something solid and angular, but at the same time soft, as if something hard was wrapped in a thick towel.

When you get to the block of flats, another person living there is just going in and you don't have to ring the bell. A coincidence that you're very glad of, as you don't have to use the key that Ahmed gave you. You still feel that you're not at home here.

That you're just a guest.

When you ring the bell at the door of the flat, no one responds. You ring again.

And again.

Evidently, the brothers have gone out.

There's no other way, you'll have to use the key. But when you push it into the lock, you find out that it doesn't fit; the door is locked. Whoever locked it, left the key in the lock.

You hear excited voices in the hall. Three, four Arabic voices, maybe even five, arguing in anger or fear or surprise, or all three together, reproaching each other or trying to tell each other something.

Why? They can see you through the peephole in the door.

'Is it you?' says Ahmed's voice.

'As usual,' you reply.

'Why have you come back?'

'Shouldn't I have?'

'Where did you leave the rucksack?'

'I was at Victoria Station, but no one recognised me or approached me, so I brought it back.'

'And where is it?'

'Here, in front of the door.'

'Take it down and throw it in the Thames!' You suddenly hear Imran's voice that sounds like an order.

'No, no, no!' shouts Ahmed. 'Come in.'

He unlocks the door and opens it.

There are five young Arabs in the hall. Besides Ahmed and Imran, there are three others that you've never seen before, obviously visiting. They're all staring at the rucksack you're holding in front of you. You don't remember ever seeing so many frightened eyes.

Imran suddenly grabs the rucksack, pulling it from your hands, and runs to the bedroom. The three visitors rush in after him. You hear the key turning in the lock.

Why have they locked themselves in the bedroom?

Maybe you're wrong; maybe you heard the sound of the key when Ahmed locked the front door behind you.

'Come,' he takes your elbow and pulls you towards the living room. 'You're tired, have a rest.'

You're surprised to see a television in the living room. Quite a big one on four legs, someone has been watching the BBC News.

A television that wasn't there before.

'Our friends brought it half an hour ago,' explains Ahmed. 'We'd like to watch a football match together. Imran is crazy about football. Just for the match,' he adds, 'tomorrow they'll take it away again. We can watch it together.'

'We can,' you say, 'although I'm not really interested in football. I can't understand people getting so worked up about kicking a ball around some grass.'

'I can't either,' says Ahmed in agreement, 'but my brother ... I can't deny him the only pleasure he has in this city.'

'No,' you agree, 'that wouldn't be fair.'

44.

What was in the rucksack?

Ahmed gives you strawberry juice and asks you if you're hungry. When you shake your head, he asks how the journey to Victoria Station went. Did anyone stop you, speak to you, did you tell anyone where you were taking the rucksack, did you tell anyone where you live?

None of that, you tell him truthfully, you spoke to no one. The journey was boring – after all, you've already ridden those buses when you were looking round London. Twice.

But the most boring part was waiting in the large station terminal, where you waited and waited and waited for someone to recognise you, since you had been assured that someone would find you and take the rucksack.

The fact that in two hours no one turned up and you had to bring the rucksack back annoys you more than anything else; you tell him this frankly, hoping that he won't take offense.

'How could a friend offend a friend?' he says in surprise, coming closer and giving you a hug.

You feel that the hug is more genuine than the last one.

'Something went wrong,' he says. 'The person who was supposed to collect the rucksack was obviously late for some reason, or he went to another station by mistake, maybe Waterloo or Charing Cross. But the main thing is, you came back and brought the rucksack back.'

'Can you tell me what's in it?' You look at him.

'In the rucksack?' Ahmed takes time to think. 'It seemed to me, and Imran thought the same, that it was better for you not to know. But now I must tell you. We are friends and so there shouldn't be any secrets between us.'

You nod.

'Like most of the refugees from Syria and other countries where war is raging, Imran is here illegally. So he can't get work. He has to survive how he can. And he does so, I'll be honest with you, by dealing in marijuana.'

'Oh,' you say, rather shocked. 'I was carrying marijuana?'

'Look,' says Ahmed, 'I really should have told you. And I'm sorry I didn't. You know that in some countries, marijuana is looked upon as a kind of tobacco. Mainly as a medicinal thing, to ease the pain of many illnesses. But here, it is forbidden. The English are very old-fashioned. Except when it comes to killing innocent children by dropping bombs from planes. I told you how I lost my relatives.'

'Except your brother,' you say.

'Now I can tell you why we sent you to Victoria Station. If Imran took the rucksack and happened to be caught, as an illegal he would go to jail for twenty years. The same would happen to me. If they caught you, an EU citizen, they would only ask you why you didn't have an entry stamp in your passport and why you're here as an adolescent without your parents' permission.'

'And why I was carrying marijuana and who to,' you add, when it suddenly strikes you.

'I'm sorry' says Ahmed. 'You would have had problems. But in comparison with the problems that Imran and I would have, they'd be minimal. The worst that could happen to you as an adolescent is that that they send you home. I really hope that you understand and that you don't hold it against me.'

'Not at all,' you reply.

From your heart. You know no other way.

For some time, you watch the news on the television.

The newsreader is talking about a regatta that will happen in two days' time. It will be along the Thames and, like every year, more than a hundred rowing crews will be competing. They show footage of rowers struggling to overtake each other, encouraged by masses of spectators on the banks of the Thames. Behind the people lining the riverbank, a block of flats suddenly appears, which seems familiar.

'Isn't that our block of flats?' says Ahmed, half rising from his chair.

'It is,' you reply.

'That means the regatta goes right past us. We could watch it from the balcony.'

'That's great,' you agree. 'There'll be no need to shove and push down on the riverbank. There'll be too many people there. There may be so many that some end up in the water.'

'Exactly,' says Ahmed.

Who is deep in thought.

Before the news report about the preparations for the regatta is finished, Imran and his friends emerge from the bedroom. They exchange some words in Arabic. And then they bid goodbye in a friendly way.

Imran comes into the living room.

'The rucksack is ready,' he says to you in English. 'Tomorrow at nine you can take it by the same bus route to Victoria. The one who got stuck in traffic today and was late will be waiting for you.'

'No,' says Ahmed, also in English. 'In two days, right in front of this block of flats there will be a regatta. More than a hundred boats, many thousands of spectators on the riverbank. Right by the water. There will be a great view from the balcony. Although the rucksack is ready, we'll have to get rid of it.'

Imran is stunned and angry. A discussion begins between him and Ahmed in Arabic, which of course you don't understand, but it's clear they are having a furious argument. Imran is trying to convince Ahmed of something and is accusing him of something.

But Ahmed is telling Imran something and won't back down.

In the end, Ahmed stands in front of Imran.

And he shouts in his face: 'Regatta, regatta, regatta!'

Then he goes into the bedroom, slamming the door behind him. Imran looks angry, defeated, lost. But still defiant.

'Go to bed,' he tells you.

You do as he says.

Ahmed and Imran argue most of the night in the bedroom. You've no idea what about.

But you are glad that the next morning, there is no need to take the rucksack to Victoria Station.

You're fed up of riding buses around London. You had a long journey to get here, you're tired, you're fed up of almost everything that has happened and is happening. The sense of adventure is slowly turning into nervous exhaustion.

And the wish to go home.

In London, it seems that your friend Ahmed is safe. Although he says the opposite, he doesn't need you anymore.

45.

Regatta

Look through the window.

Open the door and go onto the balcony.

The regatta is starting. Long rowing boats full of rowers pulling at the oars as if their lives depended on it are moving along the Thames.

On the meadow by the river, which is usually empty apart from the odd dog walker, several hundred cars are parked. A real crowd. A bit farther on, there are tables and chairs; there are men, women, children, families, grandmothers, grandfathers, people of all ages sitting there. They are drinking from plastic cups; some are stuffing sandwiches, chocolate, fruit into their mouths. Kids are eating ice cream.

Beyond the cars, along the footpath that runs beside the Thames all the way to Hampton Court, right by the river, there is a mass of spectators, who want to be as close as possible to what's going on. Some are shouting, some clapping, some just standing and watching.

You've never seen anything like it.

So much life in one place!

A certain energy, submerged or suppressed, also awakes in you. Life is still good, lively, full of enjoyment. Once again, you feel gratitude that Ahmed rescued you from the Kolpa; that feeling has got its hooks into you and you cannot shake it off. At times, it seems that it is only this feeling of gratitude that is giving you the will to live.

On the 'pig route', as Ahmed called it, you became, without particularly trying, friends for life. Your heart is bathed in a soft warmth; nothing in the world is worth more than the friendship of two people who will always protect each other.

But where is Ahmed now, so that you can watch the hustle bustle together? If you watched together, it would be that much more exciting, like a film is better and more interesting if you watch it with someone with whom you can share your feelings.

Just then, the door opens, Ahmed and Imran come into the flat – in fact they rush in and stop in the living room.

'Come onto the balcony,' you invite them.

'No,' says Ahmed. 'It's too far from here. Let's go nearer. Let's go down to the river!'

You're happy to be invited. You leave the flat together. Ahmed doesn't lock the door. When you ask him why, he replies that he doesn't want the keys in his pocket; in any case, you'll be back soon. The building is safe, no one would try to open the door of a flat that wasn't his.

You go down in the lift and then one after the other towards the exit.

In the car park in front of the building, Imran goes up to a large SUV with darkened windows. With a click of the key, he opens the door and gestures for you to get in.

'Quickly, quickly!' he says in English, so that you understand.

He gets behind the wheel, Ahmed hurries to the other side and gets into the seat beside him.

Then he orders you: 'Go on, get in the car, in the back seat!'

You do as you're told.

His tone confuses you. You'd been hoping to go down to the Thames and watch the rowing competition from up close. But Imran evidently plans to drive somewhere else, maybe into the city centre, which you don't want to see any more of because it's nothing but shops and shopping.

And how come Imran suddenly has an expensive SUV with darkened windows?

Maybe he had it the whole time and didn't want to use it.

But at the Tesco supermarket, Imran doesn't turn left, towards the city, but right, onto the road going west. Where's he going? But then he immediately turns right again, onto Ferry Road, which leads to the meadow beside the Thames, where cars are parked.

He stops at the barrier, where a middle-aged man is collecting the entrance fee. Actually, it's a voluntary contribution and the money will go towards organising next year's regatta.

Imran gives him a fifty-pound note.

'Oh,' says the security man. 'That's the biggest contribution so far. Thanks very much. You're a bit late, but if you turn right and go to the end, you're sure to find a parking place.'

'I will, don't worry,' replies Imran and drives on.

46.

Unfortunate Event 2

Look through the window.
Not the side window, but through the windscreen. In front of the car are tables where families are drinking and eating snacks.
You saw them from the balcony.
Suddenly, Imran – and this is the last thing you would have expected – loses control of the vehicle. Is he drunk? Is he having a heart attack? He runs into the tables. He drives over the tables. He crushes them, he crushes the families sitting at them, including some babies in pushchairs or in their mothers' arms.
He drives on and crashes into the crowd of spectators by the Thames, running some of them over, pushing them into the water, where there is a splash and they start to drown.
'Imran!' you yell.
How could he lose control of the vehicle?
When it seems to you that a hundred people have already been crushed or knocked into the river – men, women, boys,

girls, grandmothers, grandfathers, mums, babies, even invalids in wheelchairs – you hear a crack such as you've never heard before.

The glass in front of Imran shatters. An invisible force knocks him back against the seat.

Blood bursts from his chest.

His hands slide from the wheel, the car veers to the left, turns over and falls into the river. After a few moments, water begins to pour in.

You are drowning.

Ahmed!

The only thing you think of at that moment is that you must save Ahmed.

The friend who saved your life.

You feel the water slowly filling the car. While there is still some air available, you take a deep breath and hold it. You've often seen such scenes in films on the television. You know that you can't open the door until the car is full of water, and the pressure inside is the same as that outside.

When that happens, you push open your door, swim out, open the front passenger door, drag Ahmed out and pull him up towards the surface of the river.

When the fresh air bursts into your lungs, it is like a blow to the head. You take a deep breath.

Ten, twenty pairs of hands pull you onto the bank.

More than a hundred pairs of hands are rescuing others who ended up in the river.

You are breathing normally. You survived.

But Ahmed is lying beside you, motionless.

47.
Understanding the incomprehensible

Look through the window.

Go onto the balcony and look at the scene beside the Thames.

You are overcome by a feeling of unreality. On the one hand, you are happy because you are safely back in the flat; on the other hand, you feel as if you are dreaming.

If you wanted to describe the scene in the Book of Lists, you wouldn't find the right words.

But how is it possible that you and Ahmed are once again in the flat?

A short time before, weren't you lying on the riverbank? Weren't you part of what now, on the balcony, seems impossible?

Didn't you pull Ahmed from the car that ended up at the bottom of the river? Didn't you put your hands under his arms and pull him up to the surface of the water, from where you were both pulled onto the grassy riverbank. Where he lay without moving? Where two men intervened, turned him on his stomach and beat him on the back until he started to spew up water?

Didn't he suddenly sit up and cough for a good five minutes, while the two men went to help others who the uninjured regatta spectators had already pulled from the river and who were lying on the bank without moving, just as Ahmed was a little before?

Hadn't the activity on the riverbank only increased?

Weren't there more and more ambulances and police cars appearing from all sides with their lights flashing and sirens wailing? Weren't there divers, jumping one after the other into the river?

Nothing's clear to you; the shock is too great.

Now you remember that Ahmed, when he had coughed up and spat out the last mouthfuls of water, grabbed your hand, got up and pulled you through the crowd towards the block of flats, thirty metres away.

Didn't he say: 'Let's go, quickly!?'

Didn't he exclaim '*Allahu Akbar*', when you discovered that someone has left the entrance door wide open and even left a folded newspaper under it, so it didn't close?

It suddenly strikes you: Where is Ahmed?

You find him in the bedroom, bowing towards Mecca and convulsively declaiming Muslim prayers.

How would you describe his tone of voice?

It seems to you a mixture of fear, gratitude, regret, hatred, disappointment, astonishment, horror, pleasure and guilt. All the feelings that dwell in the human soul.

If not in the soul, then there where feelings hide.

He doesn't see you, he doesn't hear you. Absorbed in a convulsive ritual, which it is difficult to say represents thanks or reproach.

But you can't reproach God for anything, it seems to you. God knows what he is doing and why; you can only be grateful to God that things are not even worse.

He suddenly rises onto his knees, looks at you with dim eyes and almost shouts: 'What's wrong with you? Take off those wet clothes, have a shower, rub yourself with a towel, clean off the dirt from the river, put something dry on, what's the matter with you?'

Then he once more bends over and continues praying.

What's the matter with you?

Yes, what is it?

The confusion in your head is too great for you to know.

You go into the living room and turn on the television. The confusion deepens. On the television screen you see exactly what you can see from the balcony. You hurry to the balcony and compare the two scenes. The one by the river is slightly different from the one on the screen.

The television pictures are accompanied by a commentary.

Someone is explaining what is happening

The camera is moving among the bodies on the riverbank, among the wounded that are being placed on stretchers and taken towards ambulances, among the police and special officers who are supervising the operation, among the survivors, who still haven't got over the shock, among the seriously injured, lying all around, who medical staff are trying to revive.

There follows an interview with someone in police uniform, who says that no one was expecting this. That 'we have experienced the worst ever terrorist attack in London'. That it's still not clear how many fatalities there are and how many injured, but that there are a lot of children among them, including babies.

And that one of the police officers protecting the spectators had shot the driver of the terrorist vehicle and it had driven into the river. In doing so, it had knocked a still unknown number of people into the water, some of whom had swum to the bank, others were still being searched for and rescued.

It wasn't possible to say how many bodies would be found in the river.

Then they showed Imran's SUV being lifted from the river by a crane. Imran's body was in it.

You realise that it wasn't an accident

That you have become part of something much worse than you imagined in your darkest moments.

Somewhere inside you there is still a nagging conviction that Imran lost control of the vehicle through clumsiness, maybe because of a heart attack, maybe because he suddenly felt dizzy, which often happens to you, or maybe there was something wrong with the vehicle – after all, even planes crash because of technical faults.

Where was the evidence that Imran wanted to run down as many people as possible?

And if that really was his intention, why did he want to have his younger brother with him and you?

You feel a hand on your shoulder.

You turn.

Ahmed is standing there. His face is strangely distorted; you realise that he, too, has been watching the news report for at least a couple of minutes.

'Why did you rescue me from the river?' he suddenly wants to know.

'You rescued me, didn't you?' you reply. 'You pulled me from the Kolpa, I pulled you from the Thames.'

'You should have let me die,' he says. 'You're punishing me by letting me live.'

'Would you rather be dead?'

'I should be,' he says. 'It's simply not right that I'm not. But the worst thing is that I'm grateful to you for saving me.'

'And I was grateful to you. I still am.'

'Why?'

'While you're still alive, you can do penance for your mistakes. When you're dead, that's not possible.'

'Is there a Catholic church near here?' he asks you.

'Why?'

'You prayed with me in a mosque. I'd like to pray with you in one of your holy places.'

'I don't go to church,' you reply. 'I never have. Nor do my mum and dad.'

'Nevertheless,' he replies. 'The moment has come when you must.'

'For me,' he adds.

'I don't know this part of town. I don't know where the churches are. I could Google it.'

'There's no computer' he says. 'Imran smashed it.'

'Why?'

'I'll tell you,' says Ahmed. 'But not here. In church. Take off those wet things, dry yourself with a towel, put on some dry clothes, even if they're dirty.'

You do as he says.

You take the lift down to the ground floor, turn left and go past the Tesco supermarket to the main road. Ambulances and police cars are still arriving.

You go down a side street as far away as possible from Unfortunate Event 2.

You have no doubt that you will have to write about it under that name in the Book of Lists.

48.

Confession

Look through the window.

You see nothing, for you are in a church, the windows are too high; through the coloured glass filters dark, unearthly light.

It's raining outside.

It started to spit with rain as a woman told you how to get to the Church of the Blessed Virgin. When you got to the church, it started pouring down.

You thought that the Flood had started.

A punishment for all of us who have ever done anything bad to other people.

Or to pigs. Or other animals.

Or the rivers. Or the oceans. Or the air.

Perhaps we deserve to drown in endless waters, you think.

'Like this?' asks Ahmed, kneeling at the altar.

'As far as I know,' you reply and kneel alongside him.

'In Catholic church you have something called confession,' says Ahmed. 'Where and how can I confess?'

You tell him: only in the confessional and only to a priest. He is the only one who can give you absolution. But the priest is around only when there is mass.

He's not here now. You are here alone.

'Can I confess to you?' asks Ahmed.

That's not possible, you want to say. But something has happened to Ahmed. He is different. He is shivering, his features are strangely distorted, as if they weren't his.

You don't want to disappoint him, so you say: 'Okay.'

'But the confessional is there,' you point to the right. 'Shall we go there? I'll play the priest and you the sinner.'

Ahmed agrees.

'What do you want to confess?' you ask him, when you have both taken your places.

Ahmed begins to speak. Quickly, stumblingly, almost impatiently, as if he has barely been waiting for this moment.

He admits that he is a sinner. Maybe the worst of all those who will end up in Hell.

He did rescue you from the Kolpa, when you wanted to drown. But from that moment on, he has never been completely honest with you. He has been using you.

Abusing you.

Because he was committed to a greater goal, this didn't seem wrong to him. The greater goal was revenge against those who killed thirty members of his family.

It seemed to him right and just to take revenge.

It seemed to him right and acceptable to make use of your trust, your gratitude, your limited mental capacities, your readiness to stand beside him, regardless of the consequences.

It seemed right to him to use you to achieve his goal, because you were part of that world, part of that religion, which hates everything to do with Islam.

And because of that, because of a suppressed sense of guilt, it seemed to him right to help you in your mission of freeing pigs. With regard to that at least, he had done as much as he possibly could.

After getting to London, everything had been taken over by his older brother, the only surviving member of his family.

He should have told you what was happening.

He feels guilty for not doing so.

But he couldn't, without betraying Imran.

He sincerely hoped you could understand that. Betraying a brother is the greatest sin.

So he didn't betray him, he betrayed you.

Most of what he told you on the journey to London was only half truth, half the facts that might have made you decide not to continue with him, but to return home.

Until Imran decided that he would sacrifice you to realise a plan that he had been preparing for a year. That he had begun to prepare before his younger brother left Syria.

Before he had saved you from the river on the Schengen border, obeying something in his heart.

Imran sent you to Victoria Station with the intention of blowing up one of the buses and killing as many people as possible. Of course, you would also die. Luckily, there was something wrong with the bomb in the rucksack and you came back unharmed.

Only then had Imran and the members of his terrorist cell come up with the plan for the attack on the regatta, during which all three of you would die. Imran, Ahmed and you.

But why did you have to die, he had argued with Ahmed.

Imran, who he had to obey because he was his older brother, had convinced him that you knew too much and that you might lead investigators to the terrorist cell, which was planning more attacks.

What punishment could the Christian God hand down to him, Ahmed, for what he had done? For all the pretence and deception and the lies? For sending you to your death without any great resistance, although he had earlier saved your life?

And in return, you had saved *his* life.

'You helped me free pigs,' you say. 'My friends. And by doing that you helped all animals. At least in your thoughts, in your heart. Isn't that enough? Why would God punish you?'

'Allah will punish me,' he replies. 'I know he will. But I also want your God to punish me. I'll remain a Muslim, but I'd also like to become a Christian. Can you forgive me?'

'Completely,' you reply. 'You also experienced an Unfortunate Event. That was your brother's decision. You're not guilty, he is.'

'In France, you prayed with me in a mosque. 'Do you remember what we said then?'

You shake your head.

Ahmed reminds you that you asked him if gods can be friends.

He had replied that they can.

More than that.

'There can only be one God, even though he has a thousand names. Why would God not want to be friends with himself? A bigger question is whether people can be friends. And people and animals.'

You don't remember.

You'll have to look in the Book of Lists.

Maybe you wrote it all down. Made a list of 'important things.'

Or maybe not. You left the Book of Lists in the flat above the scene of Imran's revenge. So, you can't check.

'Forgive me,' says Ahmed in the confessional.

'I forgive you as a friend,' you say. 'Only a priest can forgive you in God's name. Or God himself.'
'Teach me at least one Christian prayer,' he asks.
You leave the confessional and kneel at the altar.
'*Our Father, which art in Heaven ...*' you begin and repeat, until word for word, Ahmed has also repeated it.
And then, because you are in the Church of the Blessed Virgin, also '*Hail Mary, full of grace ...*'
You are amazed that after Unfortunate Event 1, you can still remember both prayers.
As if they were engraved inside you.
Although you haven't been in church since you were twelve.
And that you remember in English, even though it's your first time in an English church. You don't understand how this is possible.
You kneel at the altar, praying out loud, for more than half an hour.
'And now?' you ask Ahmed, when you have finished.
'Now?' He is almost surprised. 'Our God knows. Both Gods. Who are one.'

Outside the church, twenty armed special officers are waiting for you. With masks on their faces, they look nothing like angels, but rather envoys of the Devil.
Has God lost control over the world?
You raise your hands, as you have often seen people do in films.
But Ahmed reaches inside his jacket.
You hear a sound such that you've never heard before.
The sound of hundreds of rounds of fire.
Ahmed collapses towards you and knocks you to the ground. He lies on top of you. Blood from his heart spurts into your eyes and runs down your cheeks towards your mouth.
It reminds you of the blood of your friend Piggy.

49.

What the inspector says

Look through the window.

You can't. In the small cell there are only four walls. The only light comes from a bare lightbulb on the ceiling. On the floor is a thin, dirty mattress. You woke up on it. The door is locked.

Hell, you think.

You have also died.

And here, between the damp walls, in a space barely big enough to turn around, you will stay forever.

Could Lucifer, the master of Hell, think up anything worse?

Maybe you're dreaming! And will soon wake up. At home, in your room. With the Book of Lists on the table in front of you. And all that is behind you is just a story, which you wrote down.

Sadly, it's not like that.

A key rattles in the lock and two enormous police officers drag you roughly to your feet and take you to a larger room, an office, where a middle-aged man is sitting behind a desk. The police officers push you onto a chair in front of the desk.

You notice that the man has your Book of Lists in front of him.

And your passport.

And wallet.

And mobile phone.

And a few other things that you carry in your rucksack.

The rucksack is also on the desk.

At the side, on a chair that looks a lot more comfortable than yours, sits a young woman. Brown hair, blue eyes, legs crossed, with a notebook on her knee.

And a pen in her hand.

You look at the man behind the desk. He is a mixture of all the police inspectors that you've ever seen on the television. He is most like Inspector Barnaby from *Midsomer Murders*. So you are not afraid of him. Inspector Barnaby is always friendly.

It becomes clear to you that you are going to be questioned.

'Your English is faultless,' says the inspector.

'Thanks.'

You have to say something, if only out of politeness, and that's the only thing that comes to mind.

'Miss Ravnikar translated some interesting passages from your diary for us.'

'It's not a diary,' you say. 'It's a Book of Lists. It helps me maintain contact with myself. And with my life.'

'Where did you learn English?'

After Ahmed's confession in the church, you have the feeling that the right thing to do is to be honest.

'At home,' you reply. 'For some reason, after the Unfortunate Event my capacity to learn languages increased.

'I know, Miss Ravnikar translated those passages about what you call the Unfortunate Event.'

'The trouble is, almost all my other abilities diminished.'
'Including the ability to judge what is right and what isn't?'
'I hope not.'
'Does it seem right to you to smuggle a Syrian refugee without documents halfway across Europe and into the United Kingdom?'
'You mean Ahmed?'
'We know him under another name.'
'Ahmed is not a refugee. Ahmed is my best friend. But now he is no longer. Now he is with his god, Allah. And with my, your, our God. For there is only one God, it's just that we worship him in different ways.'
'You don't say. But the last thing that interests me at the moment is the philosophising of a fifteen-year-old who ran away from home.'
'Ahmed saved my life.'
'That we know.'
'I wanted to drown in the river.'
'And then he demanded that you help him get to London.'
'No! He didn't demand anything. He wasn't obliged to save me. We'd never met before, we were strangers. And if he'd left me to drown, he'd have had a lot fewer difficulties later.'
'Him or you?'
'Both.'
'What are you trying to say?'
'When I was on the point of drowning, I realised I would rather live. And he was there at the right moment. I don't believe in coincidence. It was Fate. How could I not become his friend? Protector? Colleague? How could I not obey his orders?'
'Regardless of what the orders were?'
'He didn't want to do anything but get to his brother in London! The only survivor out of thirty relatives! Most of the others were killed by American and British planes.'

'After all that has happened since, don't you feel any sense of guilt at all?'

'Why?' you ask in amazement. 'I'm proud of acting as I did. I'd do the same again. A hundred times, a thousand. Every time, always.'

'Why?'

'Because I did what was right.'

'Even though you broke a hundred laws?'

'I've stopped being interested in laws.'

'Why?'

'Because in every society, in every country, in every system, they are different. I swear only by the laws of the soul. Which are eternal.'

'Does it seem normal to you that in Germany you broke into pig farms and drove out the pigs?'

'We didn't drive them out – we freed them!'

'In your diary it says that pigs are your best friends.'

'Does that seem abnormal?'

'It seems unusual.'

'But friendship with a dog or cat doesn't?'

'That seems normal.'

'I recommend friendship with a pig to everyone.'

'Why?'

'Only if we are friends with pigs can we be friends with each other.'

'Then I can only be surprised that you took part in London's worst ever terrorist attack. More than a hundred dead, including children, even five babies. Not to mention the injured, some of them permanently. Your friend was a terrorist.'

'He was a refugee. Sadly, no one had room for his elephant.'

'Sorry?' asks the inspector in surprise.

For some time, he is deep in thought.

'I don't know what we're going to do with you. You're under age and an EU citizen. We have informed your embassy. And your parents. Your father is coming to London. For now, you will be kept in custody. Did you know that for a month you have been listed as a missing person?'

'I don't care what you do with me.'

'You really do have brain damage, probably worse than you realise, but you are only fifteen. The same age as my son. You must care.'

'Can you return my Book of Lists?'

'We'll hold onto it for a while.'

'I need it. Only with the Book can I talk so that I understand myself.'

'Why?'

'Because for a long time, I've been hearing a voice that I don't hear in my ears, but in my heart, my soul, my mind. Somewhere deep inside me.'

'And what does this voice say?'

'Look through the window.'

'Look through the window?'

'It sounds like an order, but also an instruction, and a request. I would like to silence it, but I can't. Maybe it will disappear if I write it in the Book of Lists.'

'But you already have,' says the inspector. He turns the Book of Lists around and pushes it across the desk towards you. 'Even in English.'

You are sure that he is joking.

But no. On the last page you see something written, which really is in English, but it's not your handwriting. However, someone has tried to imitate the way you write.

You immediately see that it continues from the previous page, so you turn back to it.

50.

What you used to be

LOOK THROUGH THE WINDOW is written in capital letters at the top of the page.

And then, in ordinary letters: *Goodbye from your friend Ahmed*

You read on:

'Look through the window.

What do you see?

You are convinced that it is only what is revealed to your eyes.

But it's not like that. You see a lot more.

Did you ever wonder who is asking you to look through the window? Who is speaking to you? Who is telling everything that is happening in your life?

Who could it be?

Someone who is more than you? Someone who is eavesdropping? Suggesting things that perhaps did not happen? Is that the content of your Book of Lists?

No.

That would be too simple.

And barely credible.

It is a part of you that is talking to you; a part that was pushed into your subconscious by the Unfortunate Event and stayed there. It wants to protect you from the mistakes that you couldn't avoid after the Event. Because you now thought and made decisions differently.

What you used to be is talking to you.

Which didn't die, but only slipped into the depths, where your thoughts don't reach.

The two of you live in parallel with each other.

There is a window between you, through which you can see your former self.

And when that former self asks, begs, orders you to look through the window, it only wants you to look at yourself as you used to be and as you still are, in those inner depths to which you have no access.

You lost nothing.

Your life didn't disappear, it's still inside you, a living Book of Lists.

The world also still exists, and the world is yours.

So I ask you: Look through the window.

Not just once, but whenever you don't know what to do.

With the eyes that you have deep inside you.'

David Limon
is a translator, university teacher and researcher
into intercultural communication. He translates for various
Slovenian cultural institutions and has translated a number
of Slovenian novels, short stories and children's books into
English.